I0664900

THE ISLE
OF
CHILDREN

BY

DONALD MORRISON

Dark Forest Publishing

Copyright © 2017 by Donald Morrison

All rights reserved. No part of this book may be reproduced in any form or by any electronic or mechanical means including information storage and retrieval systems without permission in writing from the publisher, except by a reviewer who may quote brief passages in a review.

This book is a work of fiction. Names, characters, places and incidents are products of the author's imagination or are used fictitiously. Any resemblance to actual events or locales or persons living or dead, is entirely coincidental. All companies referred to are for descriptive purposes only and do not reflect the views or opinions of said companies.

BISAC: Fiction

ISBN-13: 978-0-692-94822-4

Printed in the United States of America

This tale is dedicated to a man who has taught many of us that fairy tales don't necessarily always have to end in *happily ever after.* Thank you for the many stories. Guillermo Del Toro, this one's for you.

D.M.

THE BEGINNING

A cool breeze crept out of the sprawling woods that separated Embry Orphanage from the unforgiving sea that bellowed against the cold Massachusetts coastline. An icy breath picked up passing conversations and youthful laughter, carrying the sounds on clouded puffs across the frosted air to a third-floor window where the sad face of a young boy, sat, chin resting in his hands as he stared silently at the children frolicking below.

"And why is that ye aren't outside playin' with the other lads?"

The boy who had been peering down at the others startled, turning quickly, as the soft Irish lilt yanked him from his mid-day daydream back into the room behind. He set the book in his hands on the bed next to him and watched as the young woman who had spoken stepped into his room.

"Tis a beautiful fall day Carlos," the girl dressed in dirty servant clothing said as she stepped towards him.

The boy's gaze fell to the floor at her feet as his shoulders softly folded forwards, subconsciously trying to shield himself from the interaction.

The girl paused, her face softening beneath the vibrant orange hair that peeked from out from the loosely tied bandana she was wearing. "It's not your fault boyo," she continued softly, setting her broom against the bookshelf just inside the doorway as she moved towards the bed that he was sitting on. "The other lads..." She paused, glancing down at the other children playing outside before taking a seat on the bed next to him. "Some people are just born with a wicked heart. Ye can't let it affect you so. It'll do you no good."

A tear worked its way to the boy's eyelid where it teetered on the edge before traveling slowly down his cheek.

"Oh, come now," she said, putting her arm around his shoulder, wrapping him tightly in her soft embrace. "There's no need for tears."

Carlos shuddered as he inhaled, the sadness that emanated filling the small room. "They hate me," he said, another tear working its way down the path of the last.

"Oh no," the girl replied, leaning forward. "Nobody hates you, Carlos. Hate... Hate is such a horrible word." She paused, her eyes scanning his features. "They're just different than you, that's all."

The wind rattled the window, and behind Carlos, the trees had begun to sway wildly to the autumn choir.

He sniffled again, reaching up to wipe the tears away with his loose sleeve.

The girl reached into her apron and pulled a small blue handkerchief out, turning it over in her fingers for a moment. "Some people can't accept the differences in others," she said, handing him the soft linen. "It scares them to see the goodness in those they face, because it forces them to see the faults in themselves."

Carlos sniffled again, taking the cloth and raising it to his nose.

"You're a good lad. Smart, clever and intelligent." She leaned slightly away, a puzzled look entering her features. "And you're to tell me, that with nothing but positive qualities, and a kindness unmatched, that you've gone and given reason for others to dislike you." She scoffed, shaking her head to emphasize the sound. "No lad. It's ignorance, that's all. Your goodness exposes their imperfections, and that's why they hassle you. You make them feel weak, and that's not a bad thing."

Carlos's gaze was locked to the dull polish of the worn floorboards past his bed. The young girl's consolation battered furiously against the emotional wall that he had constructed around himself. "Then why don't they like me?" He reached up and wiped away the tears that had been slowly making the fall back down his cheek.

The girl stayed quiet.

"I hate this place," he cried out softly.

His face began to fold in on itself as grief distorted his features. He had been awarded to the orphanage three years prior when the flu had taken his parents from him and from that day, he had not again felt loved, or wanted. He was alone, discarded and forgotten by all except those he shared the home with, with nearly all of them ignorant of his presence.

"Why did they have to die!?" he wailed, his head falling low, shoulders hunched as he wept.

The young girl reached out and put her hand on his back as tiny sobs rocked his fragile frame.

"What is the meaning of this?"

A voice familiar both to Carlos and the girl cracked through the air of the room like an icy whip, targeted and direct. In an instant the girl was on her feet and Carlos was quickly wiping the salted lines from his cheeks.

"I apologize ma'am," the girl stammered, her hands working feverishly against her striped apron. "The boy was havin' a fit of trouble. I was consoling, nothin more."

The voice at the door stared at her through with a cold gaze. "Return to your duties Claire; that will be all."

"Yes ma'am," Claire replied quickly, walking to the bookshelf to retrieve her broom and exiting without a backwards glance.

The woman that stood in the door was older; raven colored hair with streaks of smoke winding through in a tight bun that rested atop her head. She wore a ruffled black dress that ran her length to the floor, and spreading outwards from her chest, just past her shoulders was a laced, sequined trim that emulated a pair of crow's wings. Swirling around her, was a billowing cape of authority and an energy that crackled with maliciousness.

She made her way into the room, stopping four steps later, just between the frightened youth and the door. "And what might this *fit* you are having be about?" she asked, her voice frigid and stern. She paused, a squint shooting from her gaze. "Did you go and make trouble for yourself again?"

"No ma'am," Carlos replied softly, his gaze fighting to drop.

"Then what it is?" she snapped.

"I just..." His breath shuddered softly again as he desperately tried to keep the memory behind it contained. "I miss my mom and dad..."

"Well, you're here now," the woman replied, just short of a sneer. "You have the fever to thank for that." She paused, watching for a reaction from the child in front of her. "You can be grateful that they had the decency not to take you with them."

Carlos held her gaze; and the tears that still fought to make their way to the surface.

"The state saw fit to leave you in my care," she said, her words laced with venom. "So, you would do well to realize that your parents are not coming for you, because they are *dead*, and you should at least make the attempt to assimilate yourself into the rest of the group.

You have been here this entire time and have not once made an effort to get to know any of the other children, outside of your *frequent* misgivings. You are a recluse, and it is quite simply, unhealthy for a child to act in this manner."

Carlos felt as if someone had just punched him in the stomach; a feeling he had grown all too used to since arriving.

"I grow weary of finding myself at the end of your unnecessary outbursts." She stared at him for another moment, her eyes twitching as a small squint flashed through them. "It is most *unbecoming* of you." She paused for another moment, hoping for a retort. "You would do well as I have made known for some time now, to at least *try* to make some friends."

"Yes ma'am..."

The woman stared for a moment longer, then as quickly as she had manifested herself, turned and made her way back down the hall, her thick heels leaving a thin layer of bumps across Carlos's arms as they faded.

For the next hour he sat on the bed, unmoved from his seat at the edge. He could hear the other children yelling outside and the loud clang of the groundskeeper's bell, signaling that recreation time was over. Soon the hallways would be filled with the excited voices of playful youths making their way to their rooms. It would be dinner soon, and as he slowly allowed gravity to pull him to his side, the thought echoed loudly in his mind. *They're going to see I was crying again...*

DINNER

Carlos made his way downstairs to the dining hall. He could hear the bustling commotion as the other children piled into the hallway that led to the main portion of the building. The others rushed by him as he descended the large, marble staircase that wound to the first floor. As he walked his gaze was held to the ground, concealing the puffed red around his eyes—a telltale sign that was bound to lead to another bout of teasing. The sound of a hundred voices echoed through the halls, pressing in on his ears as his shoulders folded towards each other beneath the blue sports coat he was required to wear at meals.

He made his way past the grand foyer and turned left into the dining hall.

As he turned the corner his legs fell out from under him, and the sound of laughter rang out sharply behind.

He slowly rolled over, his elbow throbbing from the impact against the hard marble below him. Two older boys stood sneering over him. "Didn't see that one coming did you *piss-pants*?" the youngest of the pair jeered.

There was a pause as the others studied their prey. "Awww... the older boy chimed in mockingly as recognition flowed across his features, his gaze locking to Carlos's puffed eyes. "Has Carli been crying again?"

He looked at the other and then back to Carlos, who still lie on the floor. "He has... Awww, booo hooo.... Let me guess? Carlos wants his mommy and daddy?" The remainder of playfulness left the boys words and a cold malice entered. "Or did the little baby piss himself again?"

"Pee pants Carli," the other boy began to chant, followed by three other children that had stopped to watch. "Pee pants Carli, pee pants Carli."

Carlos slowly pulled himself off the floor and turned to make his way towards the dining hall. Desperately he wanted to spin, and bolt to the safety of his room, but he knew that would only serve to fuel the fire of teasing and would also get him put in front of the head caretaker yet again. He lowered his head and made his way into the hall, the jeering chants of his past mistake echoing like a war drum behind him.

As he entered the massive room, the smell of gruel and boiled peas filled his senses. Six days a week for the last three years—it was an odor he was accustomed to.

He found his way to his seat and stared at the table in front of him, the silver glint of his spoon catching his eye for a moment before his gaze fell back to his entwined hands in his lap.

The hall was a buzz of excitement. Crowded voices rose into the air as hungry children chatted loudly and shared stories about their day, or heckled others and laughed amongst their small groups.

Then the room suddenly became quiet, signaling that the head caretaker had entered.

Carlos forced his gaze to rise. The head caretaker hated it when eye contact was not made during the dinner speech and from his arrival had quickly realized that it was best to avoid things that upset her.

"So, as I can assume that you are all aware," the woman's voice boomed through the hall, "that winter is once again upon us. For those of you that are new to joining us, it is a time of study and resolve." She paused, her watchful gaze scanning the faces staring up at her, managing to check every set of eyes in a breaths time. "You will be issued one extra blanket, and starting tomorrow, dinner will be served one hour earlier to allow you time to tend to your studies." She scanned again, her hawk-like gaze touching every child. "Recreation will be cut short, and once first snow falls, you will be limited to once a week in the yard, accompanied by groundskeeper Conall." There was another pause as the quiet murmur faded out, the sternness in her gaze fizzling the words quickly." The library will remain open and classes will continue as scheduled. You will contain your daily exercise to the recreation room and may I remind you, there will be no running or playing of any form in the hallways. This is an orphanage, not a zoo." Her eyes targeted Carlos and locked coldly to them. "Anyone caught out of their quarters after lights out, will be assigned to cleaning duties for the length of the winter. There will be no excuses and disobedience will *not,* be tolerated." She paused, a squint flashing through her eyes. "I expect full cooperation from *all* of you." She broke her gaze and scanned the room one last time. "Now... let us eat."

A low murmur begun to fill the air as the children talked amongst their tables, their voices held below the allowed volume of the woman sitting at the head. Carlos ate quietly and with a deliberate slowness, as to take up the entire dinner time. He had learned that the other children stared at him if he sat with an empty bowl in front of him and his eyes locked to the table. So, he learned to pace his eating, from the moment they were told they could begin, to when they were instructed to return their dishes to the kitchen and make their way back to their rooms.

The next thirty minutes crept by with languid slowness. When the bell finally chimed and the head caretaker stood, announcing that the children could begin their migration, Carlos was the first on his feet. He moved quickly to the kitchen, washing his bowl in the sink and placing it on the drying rack before making his way to the sanctity of his room. He shut the door and moved to his tiny desk, pulling a book from within, *Poems and songs for young people*. He opened the book to the paper marker he had created as he made his way to his bed, pausing for a moment to let his gaze fall out the window. Outside the trees still swayed wildly, the wind twisting through them with a fall ferociousness. He let his vision wash over the twisting giants, to the sky beyond and gazed upon the countless stars that had begun to dot the sky. He allowed everything else to fade away and pressed his forehead to the cold glass. As he breathed in the spiced odor of windowsill dust and old glass, he allowed the sounds of the other children returning to their quarters to fully fade away before pulling his head away and wiping the cold red spot on his forehead. He turned around, sat back down on the bed and opened the book. Before he realized it, he was asleep, the book hanging limply from his sleeping grasp.

CLASS

It was the light singing of birds that awoke Carlos the next morning. He slowly opened his eyes, feeling the warmth of the sun delicately pulling the sheet of cold off of his bed as its rays pierced through the dingy glass. He stretched softly, his gaze falling to the small clock above the door. "Oh no…" He sprang from bed, grabbing frantically at his clothing in an attempt to dress and gather his books at the same time. This was not the first time he would be arriving to class twenty minutes late, and the tops of his hands tingled with the memory of his last punishment.

He pulled his jacket on as he yanked the door closed behind him and darted down the hall to the study wing; his heels clicking in a rapid succession of frightened steps. As he approached the classroom door he paused, taking a deep breath and reached out to turn the knob.

The room went quiet as he entered, the other children waiting in anticipation for the headmaster to acknowledge the latecomer. It only took a breath's time.

"I'm sorry I'm late," Carlos began to stammer, his words cut short by the sharp crack of chalk hitting the metal base of the board.

"You will take your seat young man," the teacher replied, not turning to face him, "and open your book to page twelve." There was a pause. "We will need to have

13

a *discussion* about this after class."

Carlos nodded to the teacher's back, his hands working through the small stack of paperbacks in front of him. He found the worn copy of the New England Primer and slowly flipped to page twelve. No sooner had he folded the page flat, then a hot, burning sting exploded across his left ear.

The boy sitting directly behind him had slowly reached out, the stifled giggles of the other students watching held captive, and with as much tension held as possible, released the middle finger that had been coiled behind his thumb, and flicked the back of Carlos's ear.

Carlos screamed, grabbing his ear as pain erupted down the side of his face. He spun to face the other boy, slamming his desk backwards as the headmaster turned to the commotion. The other boy released a theatrical cry, and as Carlos started to bring his hand back to his ear, pain exploded through the opposite and his head was yanked up and to the side.

"You have disrupted this class for the last time boy," the man holding tightly to the top of his right ear exclaimed as he led Carlos into the hall on his tip toes.

"He… he," Carlos tried to explain as the vice on his ear tightened, cutting his words short to a cry. "Please…

The laughter in the room faded behind the echoing clicks of hard leather on marble as the pair made their way towards the main wing. He was led down two more halls before the headmaster released the iron grip he had on his ear.

As his hand shot to the pain on the side of his head he felt a firm push of the headmasters' hand between his shoulders. "Keep moving."

The pair made their way up the expansive staircase that led to the head caretaker's office. Every step Carlos took was another stone filling his stomach. As they reached the top, he felt the headmaster take a firm grip around a handful of hair and he was pulled to a stop. "You will wait here."

The headmaster knocked lightly on the caretaker's office announcing himself politely. Moments later Carlos was standing in front of the steel gazed woman in black.

"Have you no end to the trouble you are willing to cause this facility?" she spat, slowly turning her back to face the grounds below her window. She paused, taking an angered breath. "We feed you, we clothe you, we took you in when your parents were taken by the flu." She paused again, slowly turning to face him. "You are *incessantly* late to class. You have a rash disregard for our rules and time and time again, I find you standing in this same spot, with that same pathetic look draped across your face." Her eyes narrowed as her hands came to rest on the massive oak desk in front of her. "You do nothing but cause dissidence amongst the other children and you seem to have an abounding lack of respect for those who have been employed to help you become a meaningful adult. I suppose you have some grand excuse this time as well?"

"I..." Carlos started, a small bubble forming at the corner of his mouth.

"Let me guess!?" she snapped, cutting his words sharply. "You weren't the one responsible. Someone else started it. You were the foul victim of childhood mistreatment and did nothing to deserve this?" She scoffed, standing straight as her hands flipped mechanically through the small stack of riffled papers lying unkempt in front of her. Carlos stood weakly in front of the looming desk, the engraved lion's heads staring down upon him from the two front legs, massive paws holding it firmly to the floor. The woman took another deep breath and slowly pulled the top right drawer of her desk opened and paused, looking down as a vice began to tighten in Carlos's gut. "It would seem that it has become time for more... *severe* methods of rehabilitation," she said, her voice lowering as she slowly reached into the drawer. As she stood straight, Carlos's gaze locked to her hand, and the two-inch-thick strap of folded leather that was constricted within a white knuckled grip. A shudder of fear racked his small frame and he fought against every reflex in his mind not to turn and dart down the hall. The only thing holding him nailed into place was the knowledge of how increased the severity would be, should his legs allow him to take flight.

"Hold out your hands…"

THE BEATING

Carlos sat in the quiet of the boy's bathroom, his legs folded beneath him. He winced as he gripped the toothbrush in his hand, the welts running from his wrist to his first knuckles screaming as his hand closed. His eyes fell to the still water in the bowl just in front of his face. He leaned over, the smell of porcelain and stale mildew filling his nostrils as he took in his reflection cast in the funneled pool.

The headmaster had beaten his hands with the leather strap until the first drops of blood calmed her frenzy. When she was satisfied, she then issued her *real* punishment. For the remainder of the coming winter, Carlos would complete his studies in his room. He would no longer participate in classroom activities with the other children, and during that time, he would be relieving the servants of their assigned bathroom maintenance. He was to clean every bathroom in the mansion with nothing more than his toothbrush and a small bucket of soap.

As he pulled his gaze away, he saw the drying puddle of urine surrounding the base of the toilet in the next stall; a sign that the other children had already become aware of his new task.

Carlos took a deep breath, releasing it in a series of small shudders.

As his gaze fell back to the small bowl of soap resting next to him the muffled sounds of footsteps approaching wandered its way into his ears. He could hear the sound of boys talking and as they approached he brought himself to his feet and started to make his way out of the stall.

"What do we have here?" a voice sneered, the whiny pitch of young adolescent puberty cracking off the tiled bathroom walls. "Looks like we found our new bathroom janitor."

The other boys chuckled.

Carlos held the gaze of the boy speaking for a moment before tearing it away and moving to the side to walk past.

"Not so fast piss pants," the older boy hissed as Carlos attempted to make his exit. "I got two hours of detention because of you."

"I'm sorry," Carlos whimpered as the boy's hand planted firmly into his chest, holding him place.

"You will be..."

The smaller of the boys turned and made his way to the bathroom entrance and peered cautiously out before turning around to nod at the others.

"It's clear," the boy standing next to the sinks reported as the older boy's hand balled into a fist.

"Let's see your mommy and daddy save you from this."

Carlos's stomach exploded, a jackhammer of force expelling the air from his lungs in a violent eruption.

Carlos dropped to the floor, his legs buckling beneath the weight of the boys punch.

As he curled up on his side he felt the impact of the boy's foot into his side.

"If you ever get me in trouble again."

Another explosion against his ribs.

"I'll make sure you never get up."

Another.

Carlos felt the impact of each kick rocking through him. He was still gasping, struggling to regain the air his body screamed for with each blow to his side. There was a sea of stars swimming across his vision and each gasp came harder and harder. The threatening words of the boy evoking his punishment had all but faded away.

Finally, the weight against his chest tore free and he filled his lungs with the bathroom air. He gasped, the cracking words around him filtering their way back into his ears.

"Next time," the boy jeered, "we'll leave you with your head in a toilet."

Carlos lay on his side as one of the boys walked to the corner of the room and begun urinating, his stream whipping wildly across every surface it could reach until the last empty drops fell.

"Have fun cleaning your room piss pants" the boy

snapped before turning to the others. "Let's get out of here."

The group turned and made their way out, one of the smaller boys hocking a rather thick spit against the mirror before making his exit.

Carlos lay on the bathroom floor, the toothbrush still held tightly in his welted hands.

He could feel a thousand needles fill his lungs with each labored breath and knew it would be some time before he could bring himself to his feet. He just begged inwardly that no one else would find him and finish what the others had started.

It was nearly two hours later before Carlos returned to his room. He could feel the bruising spreading across his side and each breath felt like another blow. His clothes reeked of dirty bathroom and the welts across his hands had turned to a steady dull burn.

He slowly undressed and made his way to his bed, curling up as he turned to face the wall. There were no tears left. Those had remained on the bathroom floor, and his sobs had been stifled quietly in one of the stalls.

PUNISHMENT

When Carlos awoke the next morning, he winced as he brought his hands up to rub the crusted sleep from his eyes. The beating they had received the prior day had been forgotten in the night, but revived the moment his hands began to curl. He lay there for a moment, waiting for the sting to subside and then allowed his arms to delicately lower back to his sides. His gaze was focused on the weathered grey paint chipping from the ceiling above him and he could hear the playful sounds of the other children on the grounds below, the sounds filtering through the glass into the empty room surrounding him. He lay there for some time before slowly pulling himself to a seated position on the edge of his bed. As he sat there feeling the electric tremble that accompanied a night of restless sleep, he heard the sound of something flitting against his window. He pulled his attention from the weathered floorboards to the grey, cloudy sky beyond the glass pane. He sat there, his neck craned for a moment and then crept across the bed to allow himself a protected view of the landscape below, a field of green spotted by running children and bordered by the large swaying trees that disappeared into the horizon. He stared down at the grounds for a turn of the clock, and as he was about to yank his gaze away to the stack of schoolbooks on his desk, something caught his eye, something out of place—something peculiar. Atop a log in the middle of the yard, sat what Carlos thought quickly to be an oddly shaped bird. He had to squint, but with a strain he could make out what appeared to be the body of a very small person, with the wings of a dragonfly flickering from its back. Its scales were a dull green, and from his third-floor window he could almost make out the lizard like structure of its head. He stared at the tiny, scaled creature standing on the massive trunk, unseen by the other children, and watched as it turned its head in his direction, the nearly translucent wings on its back flickering in the breeze. For a moment the two held eye contact, and then as quickly as he had noticed it, it turned its head and flitted into the trees beyond the grounds, disappearing as quickly. He sat there, his hands propped on the windowsill, questioning what he had just seen and if he was still between slumber and wake, when he heard footsteps approaching from down the hall. He quickly spun and brought himself to the seated position on the edge of his bed, regretting that he hadn't heard them sooner so he could at least have one of his schoolbooks opened and ready.

"It's no day to be shut in young man."

He breathed a small sigh of relief as he realized that it wasn't the headmaster and allowed his shoulders to relax a bit as he followed the schoolteachers eyes to the pile of books on his desk. "It'll be but a matter of time until the snow falls, and yard time falls back to once a week. Best you enjoy it while you can."

He was going to argue, telling the teacher that he had been forbidden from going outside during recreation time; that he had been instructed to stay in his room as punishment, nose down in the books that sat vigilant.

"Your studies will be here when you return," the older man said, a smile grazing his features. "Go play." The man paused. "We only get to be young once, you'd find it wise to enjoy it while the time is here. Trust me on this."

Carlos nodded again, holding his tongue as he watched the teacher turn and make his way back down the hall, disappearing into the echoes of fading steps.

He knew the headmaster had strictly forbidden him from recreational activities, and that a teacher unaware of his punishment suggesting that he go outside was no excuse to disobey, but the teacher was right, and he would have the rest of winter to study, when he wasn't scrubbing the grime from the communal bathrooms.

He sat there for a moment, the security of his room and studies pleading with him to stay, his sense of right and wrong tingling at the back of his mind. Slowly, mechanically, he rose to his feet and pulled the light wool jacket off the back of his desk chair, taking a deep breath and turning to make his way into the hall. As he slowly walked towards the staircase at the end of the corridor that led to the main foyer and the grounds beyond, his mind wandered back to the strange creature he had seen. He convinced himself that it must have been some type of bird he had never seen before, or an abnormally large insect, or image conjured up by a lasting dream. Things like that weren't real, and there had been other children running and playing around it, so had it truly been there, surely, one of the other children would have taken quick notice and alerted the others to the strange creature's presence. No... It had been his imagination. He was sure of it.

He opened the main door to the mansion and was greeted by a soft gust of fall chill. He reached up and pulled his collar upwards and put his hands in his pockets as he made his way down the front steps. He stopped for a moment, glancing at the massive log which lay boding and still, spanning thirty feet of the yard, the only thing that had been either too massive to move, or too low on groundskeeper Connal's priorities to worry about. He scanned the giant trunk and then turned to make his way to the back of the estate with a small shake of his head. As he made his way around to the backside of the building, he was reminded of why he always found himself there. The grounds were quiet. Nearly all of the children stayed in the front where the swings and activities were, huddled in their little packs, frolicking and teasing each other. Behind the orphanage, however, it was peaceful, a solitude he could escape to with a book, or his youthful daydreams.

He slowly exhaled, watching as his breath formed a smoky cloud in front of him. He pretended for a moment that he was a dragon, preparing to breathe fire and then smiled as he turned the corner. He made his way towards the trees to his favorite secluded spot; a large flat rock that was just at the edge of the clearing. It was his throne, his magic carpet, the Spanish galleon he was captain of, but mostly it was where he would spend his spring and summer days laying under the warm sun, watching the treetops sway gently above him. Today however, it was just a rock.

Carlos climbed atop the massive stone. He slowly adjusted and then lay on his back, his gaze wandering through the trees to the dark grey clouds forming above. He crossed his arms over his chest and put his hands into the warmth of his armpits as he stared at the slowly shifting shapes above. The air was cool, creeping to chilly, and for a moment he felt his body relax, the sound of rustling leaves and creaking branches carefully lulling him into an afternoon nap.

He had been on the rock for some time, the fall sounds having lured him to sleep, the thin wool of his jacket protecting him from the November air. He didn't notice the voices approaching him until the sound of laughter was nearly upon him, piercing and loud, a violent contrast to the brushing breeze and distant bird chirps that had been dancing through his dreams.

He sat up, blinking as his eyes focused on a small group of children approaching. He quickly wiped the thin streak of drool away with his sleeve and realized as he brought his arm down that the laughter was coming from two young girls and the three boys that he had fallen prey to many times in the past. As his eyes fell to the boy who was the self-proclaimed leader of the pack, the giggling stopped.

"Why are you hiding all the way back here piss pants?" the boy jeered, looking to the others for approval of his wit.

"I wasn't hiding," Carlos stammered softly in return, his gaze shooting quickly between the group and to the orphanage behind. "I... just like it here."

"Well then I guess we'll like it even more then," the boy said, stepping towards him after shooting a quick glance to the others. "This is *our* spot now." He reached out and grabbed the front lapel of Carlos's coat, pulling him towards him. Carlos attempted to stand and move forward at the same time but lost his footing and fell hard to the ground at their feet, the soft sound of fabric tearing as he landed in the dirt.

"Oops," the boy said, staring down at him with a cruel grin. "Looks slippery," he added, throwing a smile to the others. "Better be careful climbing up."

Carlos clutched at his stomach and could feel the onset of tears beginning to well up behind his eyes. He couldn't cry. He couldn't show weakness. Those were things he had learned that only made it worse. He slowly caught his breath and brought himself to his feet, turning to make his way away from them.

"Wait," the other boy said as he was attempting to pass. "Looks like piss pants here tore his jacket." He paused, shooting a malicious grin to the older boy and girl who had already made their way onto the massive slab. "Let me fix that for you."

The boy reached out and grabbed Carlos's jacket with both hands and jerked hard in opposite directions, ripping the fabric from his armpit to the base of the coat. The jacket flayed open. "That's better," the boy laughed. "Now there's ventilation."

Carlos felt his hands tingle as his mind conjured up all manner of things he was incapable of bringing himself to say and things that he could never physically accomplish against them. Instead he looked down at his jacket and held his tears. He refused to show weakness. He looked down and could see where his shirt was untucked and felt the cold pressing in on him. His only desire was to escape, so he turned and started quickly towards the mansion and the safety of his room. The cold air tightened the skin under his torn jacket, and he quickened his pace. He knew he was going to be punished for ruining his jacket, he just hoped that he could keep it hidden for as long as possible.

As he made his way up the front steps all hopes of postponing disappeared and an icy chill ran through his veins, colder than any Massachusetts wind. At the top of the stairs was the head caretaker. She had already seen the damage to the coat before he had even realized she was standing there and as he looked up, he knew there would be no escaping.

"What have you done to your clothing? And why are you out here when I *strictly* forbade you from leaving your room?"

Carlos could feel fear stabbing deep into him.

"I... I'm sorry. Mr. Rivers told me I should come out..." His reply came weak and stuttered. He knew that no matter what he said, his words would be taken at minimum as a lie. He desperately wanted to scream that the other boys had done it; that he had been minding his own business when they had come and destroyed his jacket so that they could take his spot. He wanted to tell her everything, but he knew that his words held no value to her, and that the punishment that would come from *them*, when they found out he snitched, would be far worse than anything she could exact. "I fell climbing a tree," he lied, his little mind racing as fast as it could to come up with a viable explanation for the massive gash in his only coat. "It was an accident."

"You have not only destroyed the coat we were kind enough to lend you," she snapped at a low growl, "but you have the nerve to stand there and lie to my face." She paused, her skin flushing red in the cold with anger.

"I... I'm not lying, I swear. I was climbing a tree out back and my foot slipped. I got caught on a branch as I fell. I'm sorry."

"Inside, *now*," she hissed.

As he crossed the main entrance a feeling he had grown all too familiar with filled his gut, a thought that seemed to hold residence inside of him. *I should have stayed in my room.*

Carlos had spent the last three years growing all too aware of that sensation. In an orphanage filled with predominately white children, his light brown tone had caused ripples to say the least, from the beginning. And it had been to the immediate relief of the two fresh off the boat Irish children when he had arrived, the spotlight now moving to an even more approachable target. It was the day he had his *accident*, however, that set him on a course of ridicule and abuse, and it was that moment for some reason that his mind seemed to wander to as his shoes clicked down the vastly empty corridor.

A solitary hand lingered in the air, fingers twitching

in desperation. Ten-year-old Carlos trembled beneath it, his legs pressed together, moving slightly from side to side as the contents just above threatened to burst free. His eyes were affixed to the back of the schoolmaster's shirt as she wrote her deceptively difficult multiplication problem on the board. It seemed an uncountable amount of time that her back was to him, every second crawling by as the muscles in his legs began to quiver. He knew better than to call out; disruption in the classroom was untolerated, so he held his tongue. It was an eternity of pressure and anxiety before she finally turned to face the class, her eyes settling on his outstretched hand.

"Yes Carlos," she asked, arduously slow.

"May I please go to the bathroom?"

There was a painfully long pause.

"Be quick young man," the teacher replied. "The class will be waiting for your prompt return."

Carlos folded his book and stood, making his way to the doorway as quickly as he could when he felt the warmth making its way towards the floor inside his pant leg. She hadn't turned in time.

It was seconds before the other students began to notice.

"Carli peed his panths!!" A boy with a strong lisp in the front row announced to his fellow classmates in glee, basking in the moment that would remove the spotlight from his speech impediment and place it firmly on the newest arrival. There was a moment's pause as Carlos froze in place, the remainder of his bladder making its way to the tile below and the entire classroom erupting in waves of rolling laughter. He curled into himself, tears already beginning to salt his cheeks.

"Dear god!" the teacher exclaimed from the safety of her desk. "Go to the servant's quarters, retrieve a mop and clean that mess up immediately."

"Pee panths Carli, pee panths Carli, pee pants Carli..."

The chant reverberated as he entered the hall, piercing chagrin coursing his veins like vile acid, the warmth down his waist turning to a low, tingling burn as the teacher's voice eventually rose above it calling for the children to settle down.

When he returned, the entire class stared at him with a giant, wicked conjoined grin as he mopped his shame from the floor. Eyes like daggers cut through him as they made exaggerated faces of disgust and held their noses. The front of his pants were still soaked and he knew at that moment, looking into the joyful eyes of the boy with a speech impediment, that it was something that would never be forgotten.

"It would appear that your *learning disability* is also accompanied by an avidity for not telling the truth." The head caretaker's words cracked through the air a short time later, slapping him across the cheek, bringing him quickly back to the empty hallway.

"But," Carlos began, his words immediately cut short as they entered the headmaster's office.

"The lesson you are about to learn, Mr. Aguilar, is one you would do *well* to remember." Her eyes moved past him to the servant girl mopping in the hallway. She motioned for the girl wearing the neatly tied bandanna with a slight nod and curl of her fingers.

Carlos held his gaze straight.

"Miss O'Connor," she said as the girl entered the room quietly. "You will escort Mr. Aguilar here, back to his room, where he will be spending the remainder of the week, with his door locked." Her serpent gaze crept down to meet his. "Maybe," she hissed, a venomous sting accompanying her words, "this will give you time to reflect on the decisions that you have made, and the course of your further actions while you are here at Embry."

Carlos stayed quiet, a trembling chill running through his fragile frame.

"Miss O'Connor," she said, her eyes falling to the stack of papers on her desk as she reached out and began organizing them into orderly stacks as if the room had been empty the entire time.

"Oh Carlos, me boy," the young servant accompanying him to his punishment said softly as they walked. "What've ye done this time?"

"It wasn't me..." Carlos replied in a soft whimper. "It's never me."

The girl stayed quiet for a moment.

"I think we'll be takin' the long way to the wing."

Carlos dropped his gaze to the marble moving slowly past his feet. It was the same every time. Another of the children would pick on him, tease or hurt him, and always, always, it would only be his reaction that was witnessed. To the teachers and headmaster, the other children were saints, and he was a compulsive liar with a diversion to authority. It seemed that no matter what happened, he would be endlessly to blame. It was his curse.

"Ye really need to ignore it boyo," she said, breaking the rhythmic silence of the footsteps. "I know it's not easy, but sometimes, the best way to get even at those around you, is to ignore their vile ways."

Carlos stayed quiet, pulling his attention back to the one person who took notice of him.

"When my family emigrated here from Ireland ten years ago, we went through exactly what you're going through now." She paused, their feet clicking against the tile with a soft echo. "Our situation, might have been a wee bit for worse however."

Carlos broke his stare and glanced up at her.

"There were tens of thousands of us, all emigratin'

to this great country, this land o' opportunity as it was said." She paused, taking a deep breath. "The land itself was and is truly wonderful. The people however, hated the fact that the Irish were comin' in droves. They hated us."

"What did you do?" Carlos asked, breaking his quiet reserve.

"That's the thing lad," Claire said, smiling down at him. "We did notin'. Twas the problem. We were simply different." She took another breath, turning the last hallway that led to the dormitory. "People don't take kindly to things that are different, or to that which they don't understand. People fear what they don't know. And you lad, are different. You're smarter than the other lads, and that scares them. Your skin is darker, and they understand that because they outnumber you, that they hold power over you. In reality lad, they're no better than ye. They seem to have forgotten that they're stuck here as well." She stopped, turning to face him as she leaned down and placed her hands on his shoulders. "You have to ignore it. As long as you allow their cruel ways to have an effect, they will never stop." She leaned even closer, her gaze piercing into him. "The only thing that allows them to continue punishin' ye, is you."

Claire stood up straight and smiled, a gesture that faded the moment she looked to the door at the end of the hall. "Now let's get on with it."

Carlos stepped into his room, his gaze moving to the stack of books on his desk.

"Please think about what I've said lad," Claire said, stopping as she reached out to close the door. "Now I'll be back to check on ye in a wee bit. Until then…"

Her gaze fell to the floor, and she slowly closed the door, turning to make her way back to the main wing, her light steps lapsing into silence.

Carlos stared at the door as it closed, and the faint click of the lock engaged. He stood there silently for the next few minutes before making his way to his bed, her words repeating again and again in his mind. For the next four days his already small room pressed in on him. His bathroom breaks were regulated, and his meals were served cold, being brought to him after all the others had finished eating. As much as he enjoyed the solitude his room offered, by the last day his tension was palpable.

When the door to his room opened up, the moon was sitting brightly in the sky, thick ribbons of cloud trailing past. The silver light bathed the grounds below and turned the woods beyond into an gothic painting. Carlos was staring at the somber landscape when the click of the lock behind him quickly caused him to spin to a seated position on the bed. Claire's smiling face shined across to him and instantly he knew his punishment had ceased.

"Your sentence is up me boy," she said, swinging the door wide and bowing deeply with her hand extended.

Carlos strained to smile.

"Have ye had time to think about what I had told ye?"

Carlos nodded. He had plenty of time to think about many things while locked in confinement. He thought about his parents, every foul moment spent at the orphanage and what he would do when he was finally old enough to leave. He thought about the cruel things he would love to do to the other children and how the building would look when reduced to ashes. He had had time to think alright, plenty of time.

"Good. Then let it serve to make sure ye never end up in this situation again, shall we?"

"Thank you, Claire."

"You're welcome, Carlos," she smiled in return. "Now stay outta trouble will ye?"

Carlos nodded, accompanied by a feigned grin as the servant slowly closed the door and made her way back down the hall. He stood staring at the closed portal for a moment before turning to take in the cold comfort of his room, knowing that the door was no longer sealed.

He made his way back to the bed and let his gaze fall back out the window. The next morning, he would feel the soft grass against his feet again.

He took a deep breath and exhaled, and as he did,

the window he had moved to fogged up. As his beaded breath spread across the window he caught movement. He paused, straining to look through the frosted glaze before reaching up and wiping it away with the sleeve of his shirt.

Down in the yard, sitting atop the log, was the same creature he had seen the week prior. It sat on the wooden spire with its legs folded underneath it, staring up at him as it chewed on s small object that was held in its tiny grasp. Its head twitched, cocking mechanically to the side in the same manner as a dog hearing a sound for the first time.

Carlos stared. There was no way he could hallucinate the same thing twice.

The creature paused, its gaze dropping in the direction of the manor's entrance. It held its attention there for a moment before dropping the object it had been gnawing on, looking up to Carlos for a moment and then flitting backwards into the trees towards the ocean.

Carlos stared at the spot it had exited for a moment before groundskeeper Connal's lantern light stole his gaze.

He watched the groundskeeper walk the perimeter of the tree line and when he disappeared behind the mansion, Carlos finally turned to sit on his bed.

He brought his hands to his sides and pressed down, happy to feel the give of his mattress. He looked with relief to the stack of books on his desk and the oil painting of Jesus's face above his door. He was relieved to be in his room with the knowledge that the door was not sealed shut. The head caretaker had issued what she believed to be strenuous torture. For Carlos, however, it was simply four days where the other children were held at bay.

THE ESCAPE

Carlos awoke with a yawn, stretching his arms out as far as he could to his sides, his legs reaching downwards, toes curled at the tips. He lay there for a moment, staring at the peeled spot on the ceiling before slowly sitting up. The clock on the wall read a quarter past nine; five more minutes passed before he pushed his blanket back and swung his legs off the bed. He stretched again and then stood, making his way down the hall to the bathroom where he relieved himself before making his way back to his room. He took a seat at his desk and opened his arithmetic book, grabbing his quill pen and ink. For the next three hours he sat, working over math problems and fantasizing about a world outside of the orphanage, and the children with their fantastical tales contained in the pages of his story books.

At twelve o'clock he made his way to the dining hall, ignoring the jeers of the older boys and found his way to his table. He ate in silence, cloaked in his newfound sense of apathy. When lunch was over, he made his way out and into the yard, the servant's words ringing like a mantra in his ears as he strolled the thick grass and ignored the headmaster's orders.

"The only thing that gives them power, is you."

He wandered blankly, taking in the brisk fall air, when he found himself standing in front of the spot he had watched the strange creature disappear into. A small white object caught his attention, and he bent down to pick it up. He turned it over in his hands, realizing that it appeared to be just a piece of old bone. Probably something blown in by the wind the night before. He lifted his gaze, examining the trees looming in front of him as he dropped the small object back into the grass, and then noticed what appeared to be an unused path leading through the woods. He was beginning to take a step forward when a spite-filled voice broke his stride. "I'm talking to you piss pants!" the voice yelled, the words ripping through the air behind his back.

He paused, trying to remember the servant's words as he slowly turned to face the older boy and two who flanked him.

"You think you can just ignore us and get away with it?"

"I think he's trying to grow some balls," the smaller of the boys standing behind him said with a chuckle.

Carlos glanced nervously between them. He repeated his mantra over and over, the knot still building in his gut.

"Oh really," the boy in the lead replied with a grin of depravity. "Then why don't I fix that for him." The boy swung his foot out hard, landing it directly into the front of Carlos's pants.

He dropped to his side with a yelp, his legs curling

41

instinctively to his chest as his hands moved to cup the explosion of pain between his legs.

"Let's see you grow a pair now," the boy laughed, the other two heckling from behind.

Carlos's world went white.

As he lay on the ground the pain coursed through him. He felt something building inside of him that was foreign. It was pushing the pain and embarrassment aside, and it was happening quickly. Carlos felt the burning scorch of rage.

He gritted his teeth and opened his eyes with a low grunt, focusing on a fist sized rock lying just within reach under the log. He pushed the searing between his legs back and reached out, sitting up and launching the stone with every ounce of strength he could muster at the boy standing over him. There was a crack as the rock landed squarely against the boy's forehead, followed by silence before the stone landed with a heavy thud against the earth. Then blood started to appear.

He sat there, a feeling of relief he had never known flooding into him as the three boys stood shocked and the other fell backwards, blood now flowing from a large gash in his head. One of the other boys screamed and turned to run while the other stood frozen in place, his skin turning white as he looked down upon his idol lying motionless in the grass.

Carlos yanked his gaze away from the still boy and

saw the other approaching the head caretaker hysterically. He watched as her gaze locked to him, her eyes widening at the site of the child bleeding on the ground. He knew the line that had always been hinted at had now been crossed. Fear returned.

The head caretaker called out to another adult that was watching the grounds and together they started making their way quickly to where Carlos and the other boy were. Panic filled his chest. As the other adults were halfway across the yard, a large group of children following like a pack closely behind, Carlos forced himself to his feet and turned, darting as quickly as he could down the dilapidated path. He heard yelling as he disappeared into the trees, struggling to keep focus on the path that faded in and out. He had no idea where he was going, but what he did know was that in that instant, his life at the orphanage would no longer be the same.

After a short while he slowed to a walk. His breath was hot and heavy, his lungs burning as sweat ran down his back. He could hear the shouting of other boys behind him drawing closer and glanced back quickly before turning his pace to a jog. Trees flew past, whipping him across the chest and face. He blocked out the sting and continued as fast as he could until a short time later, he emerged from the tree line onto a small beach. He stopped in his tracks, his gaze falling upon a small rowboat that was pulled onto the rocky shore a short distance away. He glanced to his right and left and realized that the beach section only ran for half the length of the mansion yard and that the only way out was back down the path with the approaching voices. Dense woods blocked any other escape as thick trees stood, branches interlocked behind thorn covered brush. He stood staring as the sounds drew closer. Without thinking he ran to the small boat and pushed as hard as he could, freeing it from its sandy clutches and into the slowly rolling waves. Frigid water stabbed against his legs as he pushed the boat outwards, chilling him from the waist down as he struggled to climb aboard. He could hear the yelling approaching, and no sooner than he had clamored into the rickety vessel, than a group of older boys blasted out of the trees. "You're dead!" one of the boys yelled, looking frantically across the shore for some method of retrieval. "That was my brother you little shit!"

Carlos grabbed at the two oars and began pulling as hard as he could, moving slowly out to sea.

One of the boys reached down and grabbed a rock, cocking back and hurling it at the escaping vessel.

Carlos heard the splash as the projectile landed heavily in the water just past the boat.

Moments later he heard a loud crack, and his vision exploded into a sea of star covered white.

THE VOYAGE

When Carlos finally awoke, the midday sun was beating down upon him. The ocean breeze ran a chill through his wool coat straight to his bones, the tear at his side an open window for the cold ocean air. He sat up slowly, pain filling his skull and shooting out in all directions. On all sides was a sea of blue. There was no land in sight, only an endless sky, and a gentle salted breeze.

"Oh!" he groaned, pressing his eyes closed and slowly bringing his hands up to feel the dry, crusted blood that was drying beneath his hair. His head pounded, every pulse of his heart beating against the inside of his skull. He opened his eyes and looked down into the boat. Just between his feet was a fist sized rock, the small stone that had opened the split along his scalp. He pulled his gaze away and let it fall to his lap, the rolling motion of the sea gently swaying him back and forth. He sat there, the events that had unfolded running over and over in his mind. He could never go back to the Embry estate, not now—that was the one thing that was no longer a question. And even if he wanted to, he had no idea which direction it was. There was nothing but water surrounding him to the horizon on all sides. He pondered how badly he had injured the other boy. Had he killed him? What was he supposed to do now? Would the police be looking for him? The questions loomed just behind the droning pain.

"What have I done?" he whispered aloud to himself. "Why couldn't they just leave me alone?"

He paused, a scream tearing its way out of his throat as the familiar feeling of rage boiled back. "I HATE YOU!!!!"

His release fell upon the empty waves carrying the small boat.

For the next day and a half, he floated alone in the tiny boat, the endless rocking accompanied by silence, the sea taking him to its own destination. It was two days before hunger overcame him and he found himself curled into a ball in the base of the boat, the current pulling him further and further away.

THE ISLE OF CHILDREN

Carlos stirred as the sound of waves rolling against a rocky shore pulled him from his exhausted slumber. Above a lone gull drifted past, a single caw proclaiming its presence. As he lay in the boat, stomach aching, he stared up at the sky, the sound of the boat scraping lightly against the pebbles on the shoreline filling his ears. He rubbed his dry, crusted eyes and watched the unshifting blue overhead, feeling the sharp pain of hunger flashing angrily through his gut and the burn of his sun blasted face. He knew by the sound that he had arrived wherever it was that the ocean had seen fit to take him.

He lay there for another few minutes, gathering the last reserves of his strength to painfully rise to the small bench. When he was seated his gaze fell to the towering wall of pines a short distance up the shore. He had arrived on the shore on what looked to be a large island. He heard another squawk from the watcher circling overhead and craned his neck upwards to see the white and black voyeur float past. His breath fell shallow as he stared at the beach in front of him. His skin burnt and he felt as if his clothing had somehow become brittle and course along his arms and back. He took a deep breath, ocean air filling his lungs and shifted his gaze to a flicker of movement near the tree line. Floating in the air like a hummingbird twisted by darkness, was the tiny creature from the orphanage. It hovered in place for a moment, long enough to make eye contact and then turned, flitting quickly into the woods beyond. Carlos stared for a moment where the creature had been, a puzzled unease worming its way into him, and then noticed the tiny strip of trail that led inwards. He held his gaze a few seconds more before the sound of his stomach growling forced him up and he brought himself unsteadily to his feet.

He struggled to climb out of the rocking boat, dancing dangerously with what little balance he could muster as he did. Less than gracefully, he found his way onto the shore while still pondering what the tiny creature could be. He took one step and then stopped, panic building inside him as every muscle in his body tensed at the thought that the boat had somehow managed to make its way back to the same beach he had escaped from, and that he was going to make his way through the trees and see the headmaster flanked by the orphanage lying in wait. As he slowly made his way up the beach to the small opening leading into the forest he gazed upon the massive woods, and the secret portal that led inwards. He paused, his eyes widening, the voyage on the sea, his hunger and the pain he felt behind his eyes fading instantly as he shot his head back to the boat, and then up and down the beach. After catching his breath, he slowly turned back around and began down the path that led inwards.

He followed the trail for nearly an hour before it widened out and the treetops peeled back to let the sky show through. He had relaxed considerably when he realized that there was no way that the weather would be this warm if he was still in Massachusetts. He was already beginning to work up a thin sweat under his torn jacket, and that was something that would not have happened so quickly, especially with fall approaching.

He continued onwards, the light chirping of birds filling his ears, and the smell of lush foliage dancing past on the breeze. He began to forget about the journey, the stabbing pain in his gut and the small, dragon-faced creature with wings. He found himself mesmerized by the beauty around him. The path he was walking was lined with massive trees, reaching up to a distant canopy, and giant ferns, shimmering droplets of dew spread across them. The woods were a spanning palate of lush greens and dense browns, with a velvet layer of moss covering the trunks of fallen giants and the massive stones that dotted between. He watched as the cloud filtered sunlight danced through the forest mist in shimmering rays, casting millions of tiny spotlights across the wooded floor. The smell of oak and peat, layered with drying leaves and wet soil filled his nostrils and he could hear the light chorus of chirping and distant howls over the soft crunch of his footsteps along the path. All around him the heavy air seemed to wrap him in a thick blanket of moist warmth.

It was a short time later that a familiar sound wafted past his ears, perking up a sense of curiosity and rebounding fear. It was the sound of a child's laughter.

Carlos stopped in his tracks. He tilted his head to the side and listened intently, his ears straining past the forest ambiance. He could hear the birds that had been accompanying him on his trek, and the soft whisper of the cool fall breeze wafting through spanning branches of the oak giants. Then he heard it again. The sound rang clearly, undeniable. Instantly his heart began beating faster, his pulse racing with the renewed fear that he was about to face punishment unimaginable, and quite possibly be sent to a juvenile correction facility or the military. He stood there frozen for a moment before uprooting his feet and slowly making his way forward. There was nowhere else he could go.

The next three minutes, and two dozen steps crept by arduously, before he saw what appeared to be the end of the woods, and sprawling grass beyond. As he approached, the sounds of laughter increased, and he could hear the sounds of other children joining in. He reached the edge of the trees and stopped, staring at the foreign sight spread out before him.

A short distance away, standing in the middle of the

massive clearing, was a giant castle. It was bigger than anything he could have ever imagined, towering in comparison to the orphanage. There was a giant round turret on the front side facing him, and everywhere he looked, round, spike-tipped spires reached up to the spotted blue above. Standing out in the middle was a large square section with a circular tower reaching three stories high. The entire castle was constructed from faded grey brick and the roof was dark slate, the tops of the turrets the same. It was a portrait, contrasting against the pristine sky overhead. He had never seen anything like it outside of the fairytale books he had been shown as a child, and the ones he would sneak unnoticed at the orphanage.

He stared at the sprawling structure for another three breaths and then let his gaze fall to the yard spread out around it. He could see children running and playing, a group playing tag and another kicking a ball between them. It was a completely different scene than at Embry. These children seemed to be completely without care, running of their own fruition and none of them huddled in their own unique groups. He watched the children frolicking in the yard, and then noticed a slightly older boy walking in his direction from the castle. He tensed as he realized the other youth's gaze was locked securely to him as he made his way closer. He stood frozen in place, watching as the other boy approached.

"You must be the one who just found the island," the boy said as he walked up. "You look famished."

Carlos stared at the boy, fear and apprehension still clinging desperately to him as the next three seconds flashed by in a barrage of unasked questions.

"Well, anyways," the boy continued, unmoved by Carlos's reserve. "I'm Jack. Welcome to the Island."

Carlos stayed quiet, his face scrunching to a puzzled expression. *Island...?* Then he broke his silence, pushing aside the unspoken line of questioning that was still growing as the boy slightly older than him stood there. "Where am I...?"

Jack smiled as he answered, his tone chipper and informative. "Father will explain everything to you."

Carlos stared silently for a moment. "Father...?" Carlos found himself confused beyond answer. He imagined the combination of hunger and the blow to the head had wrapped his mind in a thick veil of cottony fuzz. He felt his temples pounding and the onset of a headache pressing in from the sides.

"Please," the boy said, extending his hand to the enormous building. "Follow me, he's expecting you."

Carlos wanted to turn and bolt back into the safe confines of the woods. There was a dark sense of foreboding that tore at his flesh as he gazed upon the castle that rose up behind the boy. He stood frozen in place, his hunger and weariness the only thing keeping his flight at bay as the thought of food and sleep clawed at him.

"It's ok," the boy said, his smile growing larger. "You're more than safe here. This island is our home."

Carlos yanked his gaze from the gothic architecture and stared at the boy who turned and began making his way back to the castle.

"Come on then" the boy called out, not turning to check if Carlos was following.

He took a deep breath and moved one foot after another, mechanically, in forced deliberation, slowly crossing the soft field of green that stretched between the woods and the towering structure. He passed two children sitting together chatting, a small plate of fruit in front of them, and his stomach grumbled violently at the sight. The boy and girl, both nearly the same age as he, looked up as he walked past and smiled. The girl gave a friendly wave.

It was another five minutes before they reached the stairs leading up to the main entrance. The staircase wasn't tall, but wide. Where it curled outwards at its base, Carlos realized he would struggle to throw a rock from one end to the other. He made his way up, taking three steps to climb each one that extended at least four feet out.

As they reached the top of the white granite

staircase he paused, watching as the older boy pulled one of the heavy, ornately carved oak doors outwards and turned to shoot Carlos another quick smile. "Welcome to our home."

The boy turned and made his way inside.

Carlos stood at the top of the staircase platform for another brief moment before taking one last desperate glance at the woods behind and turning to follow the other boy inside. As he stepped in, he felt his breath get pulled away.

Spread out in front of him were white marble tiles, spanning a hundred feet in each direction. On opposite sides of the entry hall were two large hallways leading further inwards. There was a massive staircase the mimicked the one outside, but with much shorter steps, and a layer of deep red carpet laid above the smooth stone that led up to the second floor. On opposite sides of the staircase at the top, were two large, arched doors with beautiful, decorative carvings covering their surface, polished brass handles curving outwards from the middle. He looked up and gazed upon the biggest chandelier he had ever seen. It was ten times bigger than the one at Embry, with hundreds of sparkling crystals reflecting the light from the candles seated in the two dozen silver seats wrapping its base. The walls of the castle were a deep, slate grey that matched the roof, and there were massive art pieces hung along them, depicting people from an era he knew nothing about. Tapestries flowing with generations of family banners hung between them and he could smell the ancient cloth in the air. On each side of the stairs at the base were two giant statues of wolves lying down, their haunches raised as if poised to attack: guardians to the colossal hall. The castle was enormous—bigger even than his imagination.

The other boy headed directly to the sprawling stairs leading upwards, stopping just at the base to turn to Carlos. "This way," he said, his words echoing through the hall as he extended his hand to the top of the stairs and then turned to make his way up.

Carlos followed blankly, his eyes soaking in sights he had never imagined existing, so fantastical that the sight of it all seemed impossible. The house his family had shared could have been reconstructed inside the foyer of the castle and still left room for the paintings and chandelier.

They reached the top of the stairs, and the boy led him to the right and down a long hallway that ended at a large wooden door. It was not ornate, but had thick wooden slabs held together with banded wrought iron and a large brass handle. "Father's just inside," the boy said, his fleeting grin flashing as he stepped to the side, allowing Carlos to turn the handle and enter. "He's anxious to meet you."

FATHER

Cool air greeted Carlos as the door slowly opened inwards.

"Please," a deep, soothing voice boomed from the end of the dark, shadow filled room. "Come in."

Carlos pierced the doorway, flinching as the heavy oak sealed shut behind him.

The man speaking from a large chair at the opposite end leaned forward, the streaming light from a window edged against the ceiling illuminating his features. He was older, and even from a hundred feet across the room, Carlos could still see the soft smile and delicate sparkle in the man's eyes. His hair was shoulder length, black and unkempt with silver veins running through it. He was wearing a large cloak, as dark as his mane, and he sat framed by an outline of curled, deep crimson curtains that stood behind the small, three-stair platform leading up to his ornate seat. The man beckoned him with an outstretched hand. "Come closer my child," the shadow in its black throne continued. "Let me see what this wicked world has brought me."

Carlos stared, fear welling inside of him as he struggled to convince his legs to move.

"Please."

Carlos took a deep breath, tearing free from the spot where he was planted, and began to slowly move forward, taking in the room as he did. As his feet quietly crossed the black marble tiles streaked with grey, his eyes pulled from left to right along the walls. Separating the floor from the ceiling was a ten foot thick stripe of burgundy wallpaper that circled the entire room. There were dark oil paintings depicting various wolves in exotic settings. Every ten feet was a dull, wrought iron wall sconce, each holding dripping, unlit candles. Bookshelves and tables topped with antique weapons and relics lined the walls. As his eyes fell forward to the man drawing nearer, he saw the chandelier in the back half of the room, its twines twisting outwards and into itself; a massive entanglement of deer antlers with large, silent candles crowning the base.

He approached the small steps and stopped; his eyes now locked clearly to the man's.

"Closer," the man said, his voice much quieter. "Let me see."

Carlos moved forward hesitantly, taking each step with measure. As he approached the throne, he could see the small, wrinkled lines reaching out across the side of the man's face, and a large, jagged scar running from his jaw downwards, disappearing beneath the folds of his fur lined cloak.

The man leaned forward, sniffing the air around Carlos and exhaling with a light puff of air. "The world we inhabit can be too much sometimes," he began, leaning back into his chair. "I can see in your eyes that you are no stranger to this." He paused, extending his hand to a small stool at the edge of the platform.

Carlos sat down, looking up to the dingy windows that were allowing the midday light to squeeze its way through. Then he turned his gaze back to the man.

"My *companion* has been keeping watch on you for some time now."

Carlos cringed inside, his stomach tightening.

"I'm sure you must have seen him."

He smiled, hovering his hand over the arm of his chair. "Little creature, about this tall, flies about to and fro?"

Carlos nodded.

"What is it?" he asked softly, breaking through the man's pressing gaze.

The man stared at him for a moment, a squint flashing briefly at the edge of his eyes. "Of all the years I have watched over this island, for that, I am still without an answer." He paused, a small grin attempting to escape and then pulled back quickly. "He came to me a long time ago, when I myself first arrived upon this isle." He paused again, smirking as he did. "Previous inhabitant possibly? Doesn't matter. Now, he searches for those that are worthy to call this castle home; those that the world beyond, would not miss."

Carlos watched the man's eyes drift to the floor for a moment before rising back to meet his, a momentary pause all it took to redirect the conversation.

"I know of how you were treated prior to your arrival here. Which is why you are here. All that are here, share a similar misfortune as yourself." The man smiled softly, looking around the room for a moment before pulling his gaze back to Carlos. "This island is a, respite for those like you—those that have become outcasts, hated or thrown away from society, those that the world cannot understand." He paused briefly, his gaze falling for a half breath, before rising back to Carlos's, a flicker of life jumping back into them. "This castle is a home away from all that. We are a family here. There is no malice, or hatred. There is no envy or contempt. Every one of you share a common bond, and if you would accept, I would like to extend the offer, for you to take your place amongst this family—to be able to call this palace your home." His smile grew larger as a flash glinted behind his eyes as if he was graced with a lost memory that filled him with excitement beyond expression. "You can eat all the food you'd like, until your heart's content. We have a nearly endless supply of trees that bear fruit year-round, and a restocking supply of boars, deer and small game roaming the woods beyond. And there is a library with endless supply of knowledge to be studied, and plenty of chores to keep you busy when you are not expanding that knowledge or relaxing with your brothers and sisters on the grounds."

Carlos studied him carefully, and for a split second thought he saw a flicker of something that bordered upon anger and apprehension flash across eyes that began to narrow as he continued, the excitement gone twice as sudden as it had arrived.

"There are but two rules, however, should you decide to stay." The man paused, staring at him intently, the friendly welcome of his voice fading away. "The first; I must ask that you do not wander the unfinished wing on the fourth floor of the castle. It is private and is to remain undisturbed." His voice lowered, a frost of distrust coating his demeanor. "And two; you must never, under any circumstance, enter the woods that encircle us. "He paused again, his eyes falling to the floor in front of him for a moment. "There is a beast that wanders the woods and will feed upon the flesh of any who is foolish enough to enter. You were very lucky to have made it to the castle. I would not like to see any harm befall you, so this I must ask."

Carlos felt his skin crawl as the man spoke, a thin layer of bumps rising across his arms.

"The monster is as old as the island itself and the forest beyond the gate is its sanctuary, its feeding grounds. It will never venture past that gate, and we are never to venture to its side. It is an arrangement that was made long before my arrival." He paused, staring deep into Carlos's eyes. "Am I unconditionally clear on this?"

Carlos nodded, his eyes moving once again to the scar running down the length of the man's neck. "Yes." He thought about his walk from the beach and the time he had spent wandering through the woods on the way there. He could have been killed, or worse; eaten alive. He felt a ping of relief as he realized that he had made it, unaware of the threat that loomed in the surrounding trees. He was lucky.

As he was thinking the man noticed his gaze locked to his scar. He took a deep breath, exhaling slowly. "The world is a harsh place," he said, reaching up to pull the collar of the cloak down to give Carlos the full view of the puffed gash. "There are countless who would try to bring us harm, even here..." He paused, pulling his cloak back up as a thin smile worked its way across his lips. "But worry not. Those who have made these attempts, are no longer with us." He leaned back in his chair as the door at the entrance opened, casting a shadow of light across the room. "Now. I am sure that you are well beyond hungry, and exhausted from your journey, so I will keep this introduction short." Another tiny grin flashed past his lips. "Jack," the man called out to the silhouette in the doorway. "Would you please show our newest guest to his room?" He turned his gaze back to Carlos, his features once again warm and inviting. "You are welcome to stay for as long as you would like. I would be honored if you would make this your new home, and eventually find yourself able to consider the rest of us your new family." He extended his hand towards the exit. "Jack will now show you to your quarters, and while you get your bearings on the schedule here, will have food brought to your room. He has been here for the longest amongst the others and can answer any questions you might have, and any that should arise." He smiled, his teeth glinting in the dim light. "I'll have a hot bath drawn up for you as well. It appears that that could be something lavished, no?"

Carlos nodded. "Thank you."

The man nodded his head slightly. "I will see you at dinner then."

Carlos turned and started his way to the end of the room, where the young man, slightly older than himself that was waiting. He turned and cast one last glance at the silent figure sitting motionless on the throne, and then turned to follow the boy to his new room.

Father watched the new arrival making his way towards the door at the end of his chambers and took notice of his slouched demeanor and trouble that the boy had maintaining eye contact.

This child had been through much, he thought

silently to himself.

"He will run," growled a voice from a dark cavity in his mind, a hidden cage with a broken lock. *"And we will chase."*

Father flinched as fetid breath wafted invisibly past his nostrils.

"No," he whispered as the door closed and he was left again alone in the room.

THE NIGHTMARE

Carlos walked in silence, following the older boy down the long hallway, past the foyer and into another hall that led to the connecting corridors running to the opposite sides of the castle. His eyes grazed every surface as they passed; giant paintings lined the walls, with iron chandeliers spaced out every hundred feet, and the décor along the walls was staggering, even to his vivid imagination. He had never been inside a building so vast and for a moment found himself worrying that he might find himself lost.

They had walked for ten minutes before the other boy asked, "I assume that Father explained the rules to you?"

Carlos nodded, and then realized he was behind the boy. "Yes," he replied softly.

"And did you understand them?"

Carlos nodded again, following it up with another single word answer.

"Good," the other said as he stopped in the hall, his words flowing behind an accent that Carlos had never heard. "This will be your room." The boy reached out and turned the brass knob in front of him, swinging the door open. Carlos watched as dim light flooded into the hallway from an open window inside. "Dinner will be served in exactly one hour," the boy continued, "but as you have just arrived, Father thought it would be best to have your food delivered. Please, take your time getting settled and food will be brought shortly. This is dormitory wing, and as though there is no set bedtime, we ask that you respect others and keep noise to a minimum during the evening." He paused, as he turned to leave. "Also, please feel free to organize to your liking. This is your home now."

Carlos stood in the room, looking at the large, plush bed and chocolate-colored curtains. "Thank you," he whispered through astonishment, not realizing the boy had already disappeared.

He walked to the window and looked out. Spread out in front of him under a still blanket of blue hanging in the sky, was the west side of the grounds. The sprawling green extended nearly two hundred yards to the forest beyond. He could see children running and playing; some lying in the grass and a group holding races near the castle. As his eyes slowly took in his new surroundings something caught his attention. Sitting alone near the trees was a young girl. Her head was leaning down, and she was reading a small book that was held in her lap. He stared for a moment. From his window he could see that she was about his age, with dark brown hair dropping in curls behind her ears, hanging down to just above the pages. As he stared, a breeze blew one side of her hair free, the light curls falling in front of her face. She paused, delicately moving the strands back with her fingers and then raised her head, looking straight up in the direction of the window he was standing in. He slunk back into the room, pausing to let his heartrate slow back to normal. Then he closed the curtain and turned, making his way to the bed, pausing only for a moment to admire how tall it stood. It was bigger, and softer than anything he had ever seen. No sooner had he sunk into the folds of his blankets then he was softly snoring, not even taking notice as the older boy came in to set his food on the desk.

* * *

"Get his ankles!"

Carlos thrashed against the three sets of arms holding him against the rock-stubbled earth. He could hear the sounds of gulls cawing over the sea below and the taste of blood ran coppery into the back of his throat as he begged for the boys kneeling over him to stop. "Please," he pleaded, tears running into the dirt beneath his face. "It was an accident, I swear."

He felt his body yanked upwards, the blood rushing to his head as his hands struggled to hold up his weight above.

"You killed my brother," the older boy standing in front of the others sneered. "And now you're gonna pay."

The two boys holding his feet slowly moved to the

edge of the cliff and held him over.

Carlos looked up and could see the waves crashing in a frothy mist against the massive rocks below. Roots jutted out of the otherwise smooth face of the cliff, dotting the wall five hundred feet down. He could feel his heart pounding in his skull, his head exploding with every beat. The taste of copper turned to iron as the moisture left his mouth.

"This is what you get *piss pants*," the boy said through pursed lips, his shaggy hair blowing wildly in the heavy wind.

"Please," Carlos begged, his words swept away by the roaring gusts. "It was an accident."

The other boy moved forward and leaned down, the stale gruel of his breath pushing warmly past the wind into Carlos's nose. "There's no one to save you this time *Carli*." Then he stood up, looked between the other boys and back to Carlos, a thin smile spreading across his lips.

He felt his stomach tighten, even before the kick had landed.

His gut exploded and he felt the tethers holding him up release. Instantly he was falling. He could feel the wind whipping past, and his heart exploded into a tribal pounding as the rocks rushed up to meet him. He could see loose branches flying past, grasping at his billowing clothes, and as the rocks filled his view, he opened his mouth to scream.

* * *

Carlos shot up in bed, sweat pouring from his thin frame, his heart still pounding so heavily he could hear it echoing in the room. His mouth was dry and there were salted lines still running down his cheeks. He moved his hands to his stomach where he had just been kicked moments before, the feeling of pressure still lying phantom across the surface. Minutes went by before he realized that it was just a dream and that he was still alive. It was another three before he remembered the foreign place he was and the memory of the boat ride, the mansion and Father slowly falling into place.

He stood and made his way to the window, resting his hands on the cold wooden sill. His gaze was blank on the dark forest below, his heavy breaths fogging the glass in front of him. He could still hear his heart pounding heavily in his ears. Time slowly crept by before he let his gaze slowly wander to the sky above, and the large, full moon that was set against the backdrop of scattered stars. He took a deep breath, letting it release in a series of slow shudders. Then he let his gaze fall back to the silver woods below.

He was about to turn around when a flicker of movement caught his eye, a shadow shifting in the dark. He paused, his breath held in his throat as he pressed his face closer to the glass and squinted down to the tree line at the edge of the clearing. As his eyes slowly adjusted, he saw an outline lurking amidst the trunks, hulking and black. He stared, his eyes creating a monstrous vision of morphing shapes before he caught a flicker of light—eyes catching moonlight in the dark.

At the edge of the trees stood a massive creature, its wolf-like body hunched over, two blazing emeralds peering out of the blackness, a barely visible nose twitching lightly. Carlos stared for another moment, his mind racing at the possibility of what it was that he was seeing when the creature's face turned, its gaze locking to the window he stood silently in. Carlos froze, his body screaming to move, his legs begging him to let them carry him back into the darkness of his room, but his eyes were locked to the shimmering jade portals below. He knew it was impossible; he was over a hundred yards away with blowing wind and a thick pane of glass between them, but as he saw the creature bare its jagged fangs, he swore he heard a growl.

Carlos buckled his knees, allowing gravity to yank him down as he spun and put his back against the wall. His mind raced at the vision he had just seen, the endless possibilities flowing in a steady stream through his mind. His heart was pounding, and it was another five breaths before he mustered the courage to slowly stand and peek over the walnut sill to the grounds below. As he did, his eyes came to rest on the small cluster of trees that stood out a few paces more than the others. All that stood was the ancient pines and lazy branches swaying in the gusts.

'*What was that?*' he thought to himself as his eyes scanned the tree line below, desperately searching for movement or obscure shapes that shouldn't be. He stared until he realized that sleep was beginning to creep back into him and then slowly turned and made his way back to his bed.

'*Just dreaming,*' he said silently to himself as he crawled back into the safe warmth and let sleep pull him back into the depths. '*Just dreaming…*'

THE INTRODUCTION

When Carlos awoke, a thin line of sunlight was casting its warmth across the room. He rubbed the dry sleep from his eyes and let his gaze fall to the shimmering flecks of dust that filtered through the shifting beam. The warmth of the covers and plush pillow beckoned him to stay wrapped within, but the sounds of footsteps passing his room in the hall peaked his sense of curiosity, so he reluctantly pushed them back and sat up. As his feet landed softly on the ancient wood, he looked across the room to the small desk and saw that his clothes had been neatly folded and left in place. Puzzled, he got up and slowly approached, realizing that someone had come in during the night, washed them and then placed them back. He slowly dressed and then made his way to the window, his eyes instinctually moving to the small cluster of trees that stuck out. He smiled to himself and shook his head, turning to make his way out to the footsteps pattering by. Monsters weren't real, at least not the big ones.

As he opened the door, he saw a handful of children making their way towards the dining hall. One boy smiled and said hello politely as he passed by and Carlos nodded in reply, his response choked in his still sleeping throat. He turned and gently pulled the door to his room closed and joined the sleepy procession as it made its way down the massive hall. He could already smell food hovering in the air as he made his way silently amongst the others, the smell of fresh baked bread and sugary scents heralding a breakfast that lay in wait; foreign smells he was not at all accustomed to. He had only once before smelled such an amazing combination of scents, during his old headmasters sixtieth birthday. As he approached, he could feel the saliva building up in his mouth and his footsteps slowly increased in speed. He turned the corner into the large open doorway and was nearly bumped into from behind as his feet slowed to a stop. Before him, laid out across four massive tables on opposite sides of the room were large platters of food. There were steaming rolls with fresh churned butter piled next to them, a large tray with scrambled eggs and cheese melting across the top, cornucopias of fruit; colors blazing against the dark wallpaper behind. He stood in shock as the other children slowly made their way to the stand before the tables and took their plates. They moved down the line taking their fill and then made their way to the tables where they began chatting lightly while eating. Carlos had never seen anything like it.

"Grab a plate," the boy that had shown him to his room the night before said as he entered behind Carlos's frozen form.

Carlos snapped himself out of the daze and made his

way towards the brass stand. "Is it a celebration?" he asked as he took one of the large, ornate China plates.

"Celebration?" the other boy replied with a puzzled smile. "No... just breakfast."

Carlos stared for a moment, the overwhelming scents bombarding his senses. He slowly reached out and took a roll, delicately scooping a small portion of butter on top. "There's so much," Carlos said as he piled another portion of potatoes on his plate.

"You get used to it," the other boy said as he grabbed four pieces of candied bacon. "No need to stand on ceremony. There's more where this came from and always leftovers."

Carlos paused, looking at the boy as the soft murmur of the room began to grow. "It's like this every morning?"

The other boy smiled and nodded, motioning him to begin.

Carlos continued filling his plate, his eyes grabbing far more than his stomach yearned for and then began making his way to a table near the edge of the room, old habits still clinging tightly. He began eating, watching the other children talk and laugh as he slowly worked his way through the food piled in front of him. When he had finished, he stood and walked to the large bin he had seen the others placing their dirty dishes in. He set his plate and fork inside and turned to make his way back out to the hall, and from there, the entrance of the mansion. He began towards the warmth flooding in when he heard the other boy call out.

"Carlos."

He turned and looked back to see Jack making his way out of the dining area.

"Make sure you're back by seven," he called out. "Father likes us all to share dinner together."

Carlos nodded and watched the boy make his way out of sight down the hallway to his right. He paused, the slowly building reality working its way into him. Then he turned and made his way onto the massive steps leading down to the grounds below and the soft blanket of grass that sprawled out before him. He walked to the edge of the mansion and began working his way around the perimeter, his eyes washing over every surface. He drifted across the grass in a haze, his body floating through the yard like a moth on a breeze. He had never imagined such a place; the towering spires and stained-glass windows glinting against the clear skies. He was surrounded by the smell of pine and blooming flowers; the cold feeling of Massachusetts falls a slowly retreating memory. It felt like he had not only been transported to another land, but another time as well. Flowers blossomed, butterflies flitted by, and the smell of spring hung heavy in the air.

How is this possible? he thought to himself as he

turned the back corner to the mansion.

The walk to the backside had taken him nearly an hour and the breakfast was resting heavy in his stomach. He made his way to a dry marble fountain that stood out from the back of the building and climbed atop the circular ledge that ran around the large statue of an angel pouring water from a pitcher. He sat there for a moment and then lay on his back, the stone warming his back through his shirt. He took a deep breath allowing his eyes to close as he imagined how much nicer it would have been if there was actually water flowing from it.

"You're the new boy, aren't you?"

Carlos startled and slid backward, turning to his side as he did, nearly falling three feet into the dried leaves in the base of the empty fountain. As he slowly gathered himself, embarrassment beginning to flush through his cheeks, he saw the girl that had been reading the day before standing there, book in hand, a smile growing across her face.

"Didn't mean to scare you," she said, clasping the book behind her back with both hands.

Carlos stared at her, watching as the sunlight sparkled off her dark brown hair in small bursts, the soft olive of her youthful skin glowing beneath.

His reply was lost to the deep brown eyes staring at him.

"I'm Isabella," the girl said, pulling a hand out from

behind her back and extending it towards him.

He looked at her hand and then back to her, slowly moving forward to shake it. "Carlos," he replied sheepishly.

"I saw you arrive yesterday," she said, returning her hand and taking a step back.

He nodded, embarrassment still holding his words at bay.

The girl stared at him for a moment, curiosity running through her gaze. "Where are you from?" she asked, prying deeper into him.

He stayed quiet for a moment longer, before peeling his lips apart to speak up quietly. "Boston," he replied, his one-word reply completing his answer as he slowly moved to the edge to let his feet dangle over.

The girl spoke with a soft accent, something Carlos had never heard before. It was almost musical. "Oh," she replied flatly, her tone leaving Carlos to ponder if there was any interest in it. "I assume something bad happened and you woke up on the island?"

Carlos stared quietly as her his gaze filled with a sad reminiscence.

"It's a similar story with everyone," she said matter-of-factly, a thin smile forming as she realized her new acquaintance was struggling to process her words. "And now you."

He nodded again.

"You don't talk much do you?" she said, her smile growing.

"I just, never really had anyone to talk *to*..." Carlos said softly, his words laced with shame. "I didn't have many friends back, where I'm from."

"Oh," she replied, her smile fading. "Sorry."

"It's fine," he replied, looking up to meet her gaze.

There was a moment of silence, only the breeze moving between them; birds chirping lightly in the distance.

"Well," Isabella said with a smile. "Nice to meet you, Carlos." She paused, her entrancing smile holding Carlos in place. "See you at dinner?"

He nodded, watching her turn around to make her way back around to the front of the mansion. As quickly as she had arrived, she was gone. He sat there for a short while, a foreign feeling washing through him, a nervousness that seemed to ebb through him. He found himself smiling.

It was a short time later before he tore his gaze away from the spot she had disappeared behind and laid back down on the warm stone. Before he knew it, the warm stone beneath him and singing of distant birds had lulled him to sleep.

DINNER

The sun had already begun its downward descent when Carlos awoke. Long shadows crept across the grass; the silhouette cast by the towering pines beyond the clearing stretching closer as the afternoon light faded. He sat up, realizing in the moments it took him to rise, that he had slept away nearly the entire afternoon. The last three days had taken a toll on him, and he could feel the weariness still clinging tightly. He swung his legs over the edge of the fountain and slid to his feet, the hint of an evening chill brushing past him. He reached up and rubbed his eyes, the slight sting of sunburn whispering that he had been asleep too long. He took a deep breath and started back to the dorm. As he strolled across the grounds his mind wandered back to the orphanage. He thought about Claire and wondered how she was doing. She was probably worried sick that he disappeared. He thought about the headmaster and how lucky he was that he hadn't gotten caught. Faces of cruelty flashed through his mind and the cold embrace of his room caressed his skin with an icy touch, his hands moving to rub together as the tops of them began to tingle with a phantom burn. He took another shuddered breath and let the thought of Isabella fill him with warmth. He had never spoken to a girl before, outside of conversation forced in the classroom, but something about her brought a soothing calm to him, laced with an unknown nervousness. Something about her made him feel welcome, made him feel safe. He had no idea where he was, and through the lingering apprehension, the only thing that gave him any sense of relief since arriving had been their brief conversation. He had liked girls, sure, thought them pretty, and was even caught once staring too long at one in his class. That had led to another embarrassing situation, for both of them. But this wasn't that feeling. This was different—warm and inviting, a breath of serenity that filled him with anticipation, a feeling he knew wouldn't dissipate until their next meeting. He smiled, the evening breeze wrapping around him as he approached the front of the mansion.

He made his way to the front steps, taking them leisurely as he admired the smooth stone. There were two other children making their way towards the castle from across the yard, chatting as they did, but everyone else was already inside. He passed through the foyer, a lustrous buffet of smells filling his senses. Once again, his mouth started to water as he made his way to the dining hall. He was still reaping the rewards of what was possibly the largest breakfast he had ever eaten, but as he made his way towards the dancing aromas, he felt hunger returning.

He entered the room filled with dozens of other

children and paused, his eyes instinctually scanning the edge of the room for a place farthest away from the others to sit. As he felt the slowly tightening grip of panic beginning to take hold he heard his name.

"Carlos!"

He turned his head to the familiar voice across the hall and saw Isabella standing at a table near the end, her hand hovering in the air in a static wave.

He stared for a moment, still unsure that she was speaking to him. After a quick glance behind him he started his way towards her.

"I saved you a seat," she said as he walked up, removing her book from the chair next to hers.

"Thank you."

He was still nervous, the feeling of someone he didn't know showing kindness foreign. He looked down at the platters of food spread across the table as he pulled his chair in, his eyes grazing a large ham, steaming vegetables and a bowl of exotic fruits. The steam wafted slowly upwards, and it took moments for him to peel his gaze away. He had never seen meals like this. His past was filled with gruel and bread with the rarest of occasions calling for thin slices of chocolate cake— birthday treats when one was afforded at the orphanage. Meals with his parents had been simple and small, just enough to quell their hunger on his father's modest income. These were storybook banquets reserved for kings and queens.

Isabella watched the new boy, staring curiously as his gaze was entranced by the food before them. He was quiet, and shy. There was something about it that she liked. All the other children were noisy and loud, running through the halls like packs of wild beasts. The boy sitting next to her was different. "You mentioned you don't have many friends," she said, leaning closer to whisper near his ear. "Neither do I," she added, leaning closer as he turned to look at her, a grin growing on her face. "Most of the kids here are kind of weird."

Carlos smiled as she leaned back, the smile glowing beneath her deep brown eyes. "Is it always like this?" he asked, his words filtering through the loud murmur of voices echoing off the walls.

"You mean dinner?" she replied, an inquisitive look flashing across her face.

"No," he replied. "Everything." He paused, reading her expression and instantly realizing that she didn't know what he meant. "I mean, I don't understand. What is this place? Where are we? Why are there only children? Where are all the adults?"

Isabella felt the questions beginning to cool as they hung answerless in the air between them. She had lost count of the number of times she had formed them to herself. She took a deep breath and began to reply, telling him that she didn't believe any of them knew, when the sound of a large door opening cut the room's conversation short, and everyone's heads turned to the massive slab of oak at the end of the room.

Carlos watched as the only adult he had met since arriving made his way to the large table sitting alone near the door. The one they referred to as Father pulled his chair out and slowly sat down, his eyes grazing over the crowded hall before him. As the inviting smile returned, slowly spreading across his face, the small creature flitted into the room behind him, pausing for a moment as it bobbed in place just behind his chair before rising up and taking a place on a windowsill near the ceiling.

"I am blessed to have all of you here," he began, his eyes moving individually between the children. "As I have said countless times, society has deemed you outcasts, miscreants in their evolving scheme." His eyes continued their travel. "The world beyond this island has concluded that there is no place for you there." He paused, his eyes moving to Carlos. "But here," he said, his gaze burrowing deeply, "You will always have a place. Here, you are family, all of you, brothers and sisters, friends and companions. Here... You are home."

Carlos held Father's gaze, the last resonance of his words still echoing through the dining hall.

"And as we are family," he continued, his eyes again

working through the hall, "I would like you all to welcome your newest brother."

Carlos felt a flush of blood work its way into his cheek and his body began to shrink in on itself.

"Carlos," Father said, raising his hand out. "Could you please stand?"

Carlos hesitated for a moment, the entire room's gaze falling upon him, dozens of eyes tearing their way into him.

"It's all right child," Father said, his smile growing larger. "You are amongst family."

Carlos felt a small tap on his leg and broke his paralysis to glance at Isabella who nodded slightly to him, an unspoken gesture for him to rise.

He slid his chair out gently and brought himself to his feet, his gaze flashing to the creature that seemed to be staring at him from above. The chair groaned as its legs slid across the stone tiles. Now every eye in the room was locked on him.

"Carlos has a story similar to many of your own. He too, has suffered the loss of his family and those that he loved. His is also a story of hardship and neglect, pain and suffering at the hands of a cruel, adult world. He, like yourselves, has been rescued, brought here to this sanctuary so that he as, the rest of you do, can live free of anguish and torment."

Carlos looked quickly through the faces staring

silently at him.

"I would ask you all," Father continued, "to please show him your kindest welcome. Show him that he no longer needs to be afraid."

There was a long pause, many of the faces turning to smiles as he peered amongst them.

"You may sit," Father said, his hand again outstretched, pulling Carlos's gaze back to him.

He turned to one of the older boys sitting at a table nearest to him. "And Braiden, if you could please assign him to the work task I have prepared and fill him in on his duties first thing in the morning, that would be most appreciated."

The boy nodded deeply in reply, his eyes then moving to Carlos, followed by a smile.

"Now," Father continued, his gaze once again working its way through the faces. "Let us enjoy this honor of sharing another meal together. Let us consume this bounty with the understanding that we are blessed to be afforded the luxury of life. Let us not forget those who were not able to find their way here, and those that were lost along the way. Let us be thankful for this meal and this island for taking us in and giving us shelter." There was a pause as the echo of his words slowly faded. "Let us eat."

The room immediately resumed its low rumble of conversation as Carlos turned his head to Isabella, watching as she reached forward and pierced a thinly cut slice of ham and moved it to her plate. He stared quietly as she moved on to the steamed broccoli and sweet potatoes.

"Are you going to just stare," she said after a moment. "Or are you going to serve yourself?"

"Oh," Carlos replied, snapping out of the food induced daze. "Sorry."

He reached out and slowly filled his plate, remembering that he didn't have to take more than he needed, because there was always going to be more; and that it would be best for him to retain some form of manners in front of his new friend.

"So, what was it like in an orphanage?" Isabella asked after he finished filling his plate with a piece of sliced ham, a sweet roll and a few helpings of steamed broccoli and carrots. "How long did you live there?"

She had heard stories of orphanages but had never met anyone who had lived at one. This made the new boy even more interesting to her.

Carlos set his plate down and paused, the memories of the Embry Estate coating his stomach in a thick layer of unease. "I was brought there when my parents died— three years ago," he said, his words low and hollow. "It was lonely."

Isabella paused, giving him a puzzled look. "Oh," she said, the wrinkles across his brow instantly forming regret in her for asking. "Lonely?" she continued, quickly moving his mind away from his parents. Did you not have friends there?"

"No," Carlos replied, his gaze still locked to the plate in front of him. "There were a lot of us. But... I really didn't—the others, no."

"Oh. I'm sorry."

Carlos stayed quiet as he picked up his fork, stabbing a large piece of broccoli, as the image of blood gushing from the forehead of the boy standing over him flashed past. For a moment he could still feel the cool touch of the stone still heavy in his hand. His shoulders tensed. He had tried to make friends, reached out to others in an attempt to fit in. But that moment in the classroom, standing there soaked in his own liquid. That had removed any possibility of that ever happening. He was surprised that anyone had approached him at all once he had arrived at the castle, let alone the girl who insisted on pulling him into the awkward situation of conversing. This was still something he found himself struggling with. "What about you? Where did you live before this?"

Isabella sighed, her fork paused in the air for a moment as the smells of her house flooded back to her, accompanied by the sounds from the bustling street that had been outside her front door.

"I lived with my parents," she replied, her cheerful tone dissipating. "We're—I'm from Madrid." She paused, her brow furrowing slightly. "I actually had many friends there."

"Spain?"

"Yes."

"Oh. You speak very good English for someone from Spain."

Isabella turned her head, squinting at him as she replied. "Have you ever met anyone other than myself from Spain?"

Carlos pondered the question for a moment, responding with a silent shake of his head.

"Then that's a very ignorant thing for you to say."

"I'm sorry," he replied, a ping of embarrassment stabbing into him. "I didn't realize."

She took a deep breath, exhaling sharply with a click of her tongue as she silently forgave him. "My father was the one that insisted I study English. He would tell us time and time again, that there could be a day where we may just happen to flee to America. He had a way of being very persistent. So, now I speak English nearly as well as I speak Spanish."

"Tag!" one of the children across the dining room yelled, the sound of a slap pulling the other's attention to him as he ran from the room, another boy rising up with his hand on the back of his head to chase him out.

Carlos watched the pair run from the room and then

turned back to his friend.

"My father was from Mexico. He met my mother in Texas when he first came to America. They moved to Boston together after a storm devastated the city they lived in. He built ships. The port he was working at was destroyed. He was offered a job in Boston, and they moved there. A few years after that, I was born. He taught me Spanish and English. He always said that we lived in America, and they speak English, so that's what I should speak. The only time I would hear him Spanish after we arrived though, was if my Grandparents came to stay with us. They didn't speak English. That's why I assumed—"

"Wait," Isabella replied, setting her fork down. "If you had grandparents that were still alive, why did they send you to an orphanage, and not back with them? Do they not send you to your closest relatives should your parents die?"

Carlos shrugged. "I don't know. I asked the headmaster once. She told me they weren't able to find people in other countries."

"That doesn't sound right..."

"It doesn't matter. I'm not there anymore, and I don't know where in Mexico my grandparents live, so I couldn't find them even if I wanted."

Another group of children stood up and made their way out, one of them pausing as they passed the table.

"Carlos, right?"

Carlos nodded, shooting a quick glance at Isabella.

"John Michael," the boy said with a smile. "Welcome."

"Thank you," Carlos said softly, watching as the boy politely bowed to Isabella and turned to make his way out.

"Yeah," she said as the boy disappeared into the hall. "I haven't gotten to know many of the others here. They already had their friends and honestly, I don't really care enough to go out of my way to fit in."

Carlos turned to her with a puzzled grin. "What made me so special...?"

"I don't know. You're different I suppose."

"That obvious?" he asked with a grin.

"Oh yeah...." she replied as her eyebrows rose up her forehead, a wide grin splaying beneath.

The pair chuckled and went back to finishing their breakfast. A short time later, Father placed his napkin down and rose, turning without a word to make his way back through the door he had entered in, the tiny, winged creature hovering just behind him.

For the next few minutes, the pair quietly chatted while finishing their meal.

"What are we supposed to do with our dishes?" Carlos asked, his eyes scanning for some form or cart or kitchen entrance as the conversation wore down. "Last time I just set them on a cart, but I don't see it."

"Oh," Isabella replied. "Just leave them here. "It's someone's job to clean them."

"Are you sure?"

"Yeah," she smiled. "We all have our jobs here. Someone's is to do all the dishes, someone's is to cook, someone's is to set the tables and put the food out."

Carlos looked at her for a moment, curiosity coursing through him. "What's your job?"

Isabella smiled. "You wanna see?"

Carlos nodded quickly. "Yeah."

Isabella grinned even larger and tapped his hand as she stood. "Come on, I'll show you."

THE CALM

The pair entered the hallway. Isabella walked in front with Carlos stepping quickly behind her. As they entered the corridor that led to the right wing of the castle they had to dodge quickly out of the way as three younger children ran past giggling loudly.

"It's down here," Isabella said, a layer of excitement in her words as pride quickly began to build in her.

The pair made their way down the hall passing almost a dozen doors before they reached the end. Then Isabella stopped and turned with a smile. "Welcome to my real bedroom." She opened the door and stepped inside. As the door swung inwards the smell of ancient tomes and faded pages filled Carlos's nostrils. He slowly stepped in.

Two stories tall, with ladders running along their edges was the biggest library Carlos had ever seen. There were books from the first floor to the second floor and all the way to the base of the large arched ceiling. The middle of the room had a massive, cross shaped bookshelf with binding after binding lining its ancient wooden shelves. There was a large commons table just inside the room with books stacked upon it and two large, thin tables fitting the space on opposite sides of the large center shelves. He let his eyes wash over the room, seeing the ornate staircase that led up to the second floor; the cast iron railing coiled upwards, a serpent protecting the edge. He could smell the musty pages and his mind flashed to the tiny library at Embry, and the hours he would stay there, his nose planted in books to escape the cruelties of the yard. He felt comfort slowly fill him. "This is amazing," he whispered, awe flooding through him as he was immediately immersed in the thousands of stories that surrounded him.

Isabella smiled. The library was her second home and his words filled her with elation. In passing he had told her that he enjoyed reading and she knew that the library in the castle was unlike anything he had ever seen. It had been for her when she had first arrived. The joy it gave her just stepping in was something she had wanted to share with all the other children, but since she had taken the job of organizing and cleaning, she had only seen one of the other children make their way there long enough to smirk and run back to the sounds of play outside. She felt something stir inside at the emotion behind his words. "It's my job to keep the library in order," Isabella said in the echoless room. "I come here every day and dust the shelves, wipe down the tables, sort and separate. I can't begin to tell you how much I love it. It's perfect."

Carlos felt warmth flooding through him as he began to think about the countless adventures he was about to enjoy. He loved stories that took place in faraway lands, with mythical beasts and heroes that nothing could defeat. He had never seen this many books, and instantly knew that he would be seeing Isabella much more.

She moved to the large table with stacks of books atop it. "See. I'm reorganizing the entire library into categories." She smiled, her face filled with pride and joy.

Carlos stepped further in, letting the familiar aroma fill his senses as he took in the size of the room. He had never seen so many books in his life.

"The middle section, that's all classics; Gulliver's Travels, Robinson Crusoe, The Monk, A Modest Proposal." She turned to him and then held her hand out to the upstairs floor. "The second floor is dedicated to science, medicine and books that could be used for school and knowledge."

"This is incredible," Carlos said, slowly stepping forward into the room.

"You mentioned that you liked to read," she said with an excited smile.

"Yeah," Carlos replied softly, still reeling from the enormity of the room. "I used to read all the time at the orphanage." He paused, his words trailing off as he approached the middle shelf. "There was nowhere close to this many books there though. I could be in here for the rest of my life..."

He pulled his gaze away from the endless spines and smiled at her.

"I would have never left my room if the orphanage had this."

She chuckled.

"This is… wow…"

Isabella smiled. It felt good to see someone appreciate the library as much as she did. Most of the other children spent their time playing in the yard or lounging about the commons area playing chess or faro. This was the first time since her arrival that someone had reciprocated her love for the massive, unused room. She knew that they were going to get along just fine. "You can stay here if you'd like. Feel free to browse. I have to go to my room for a little bit, but I'll be back shortly."

"Ok," Carlos replied, his gaze wandering back to the books as his hand reached out for a spine covered in gold leaf lettering.

"K," she said with a small grin, turning to make her way out. "Chao!"

Carlos nodded quietly as he opened the cover of the ancient book. The page edges were frayed, and he could see the individual strands of fiber reaching outwards. He moved to the table and sat down, putting the book in front of him and turned the pages to the beginning. *A Dream of Red Mansions.*

He sat in silence, reading in the light of the stained-glass windows that lined the upper walls above the second shelves. He had no idea how long he was there, but when he woke up, his hands were on page sixty of the book and the room had become dark.

He slowly folded the book closed and made his way down the hall to his room. He shut the door behind him and undressed, making his way to the window to look out again. Moonlight washed the grounds in a blanket of silver sheen. The trees moved listlessly in a slow, unheard breeze. He stared for a moment longer, and then turned around to make his way to the plush comfort of his bed. He wondered how long he had been asleep and if Isabella had returned as he slid into bed and pulled the thick covers up. No sooner had they settled around him, than he was fast asleep.

THE PAST REVISITED

The next morning Carlos was drifting through the castle grounds, his stomach full from a quick breakfast eaten late. He had contented himself to tracing the tree line while lost in a haze of adolescent daydream and had circled nearly three quarters of the grounds; a two-hour trek through a forest of well-kept grass, when he looked up and caught a glimpse of something that yanked him back from the fantasy that he was playing out in his head. Off to his right, about ten feet into the trees, was what appeared to be an old gate. He slowly pushed aside the brush that it hid behind and stepped in. As he let the low hanging branches fold back into obfuscation he took a quick glance over his shoulder. The feeling he was being watched caressed him lightly, the sensation fading nearly as quickly as it had arrived. He turned back to the gate and walked in another few steps. Standing ancient and heavy before him stood the wrought iron remains of what looked at one time to be a grand, ornate entrance to the castle grounds. Iron spires folded together in a rigid tapestry of curls and spikes. Now however, they were bent and twisted by age, leaning heavy to the sides, a deep layer of rust washing their surface. He stood there silently, his eyes working in amazement over the time forgotten passage. He looked down to see where a large path had once been the main entrance to the estate, the only remnants of it the slightly raised ground now covered by an uncountable season's worth of growth.

He slowly approached, the sounds of the forest beyond washing away the vapors of children's laughter lingering behind him. He paused, staring through the twisted bars and slowly reached his hand out, the black, shifting form of glowing eyes and teeth shivering through him.

"Carlos!"

He spun as the sound of his name cracked through the air, a lightning bolt in the silence, staggering him to the side as it did. He whipped his face around to see his newest acquaintance snickering at his momentary lapse of composure.

"Wow," Isabella chuckled as Carlos slowly regained himself. "I got you good."

Carlos brought his hand up to the back of his neck, running his fingers through his hair. "I didn't see you following me," he replied, a thin layer of blush working its way slowly through his cheeks.

"I know," she smiled, as a hint of mischievousness fluttered through her words.

Carlos shook his head and exhaled loudly.

"I see you found the old entrance," she said, stepping forward to admire the rusting portal.

"It looks like it used to be the main pathway to the

castle," he replied, turning around as she walked past him to inspect it closer.

Isabella approached the gate, reaching out to slowly brush her hand across the flaking metal. It was cold to the touch and as she brought her hand away a thin layer of orange dust stayed with her; rust flaking from its years of standing in the elements. There was something magical about it, but at the same time, laced with a shimmer of sadness.

Carlos stood behind her, watching as she stared into the woods, the image of the creature standing black against the shadows flashing again through his memory. "I think we should go," he said, the emerald gaze burned into his mind.

Isabella stared past the iron spires to the dense woods beyond and the path that seemed to fade off a short distance away. "I wonder where it goes?" she asked, brushing the light orange across the bottom of her dark blue dress.

Birds chirped above them, hidden in the canopy that blocked all but a few staggered rays of light.

"The only time this gate gets opened is when one of us decides it's time to leave, and Father leads them through the woods to the boats. Other than that..." She paused, turning to glance at her friend who now wore a mask of worry.

"Come on," Carlos said, urgency and fear forming his

words. "Let's get out of here."

Isabella smiled. "You really *do* scare easily, don't you?"

Two flashes of green in the dark.

"No," he replied quickly. "It's just... Father said we shouldn't go into the woods. I don't want us to get in trouble."

Isabella smirked, letting the expression quickly morph into a tiny smile. "Ok... miedica."

"What's that?" Carlos asked as he pushed the brush aside.

"Nothing," she grinned as she stepped through.

Carlos followed behind her, the portal closing behind them as they stepped onto the grounds. She was already walking ahead, and he quickly caught up to her as she made her way back to the castle.

"—and then I woke up here," Carlos said, finishing up his story as the pair sat on the front steps to the estate, the sun hanging warmly in the afternoon sky above. "What about you? What was your life like before this?"

Isabella stayed quiet for a moment, colors of grey, blue and black entering her mind in a swirl, her mother's face appearing just long enough to make her heart sink.

"It's ok if you don't wanna talk about it," Carlos said, sensing the sadness coming from his friend.

"Papa was in the military," she began after taking a deep breath to steel herself for saying words she had never had to form. "My mama was the one that raised me. I'd only see him when he would come home to visit. I would wait months for that." She paused, a breeze brushing her hair as it passed. "He was kind." Memories of her father's smile filled her vision, and she could feel her chest beginning to grow heavy. "It was almost six months ago. Mama woke me up. It was very late. She seemed scared. I could hear papa shouting from downstairs. I knew something was wrong. He never shouted, no matter how angry he became." She paused again. "He came to my room and told me to pack everything that was important, to do it quickly. That's when he said that we were leaving."

Carlos watched Isabella speak, her hands folding into tight knots in her lap. Her gaze had fallen on the white marble steps they were sitting on, and her usual glow had faded. He could feel the sadness ebbing around her.

"We packed everything we could carry that night." She paused again. "We left behind nearly everything we owned. Pictures, books, dolls that papa had given me on birthdays... everything." She took another deep, shuddered breath. "Papa said that civil war had finally broken out. He said that the group he was fighting with, had finally decided to rise up against the republic, but the government had found a list of those that were leading that uprising." She raised her eyes to Carlos. "Papa's name was on that paper." The gaze fell back to her lap. "He said that people were coming for them, for *us*, and that we had to leave, or we would be killed. That night we were on a boat for America." Isabella's brow furrowed tightly, a grimace clenching her features. "It was three days later that the storm hit."

Carlos sat quietly, watching as the dam holding back a flood of Isabella's emotions begin to crack.

"I remember waking up to papa shouting, seeing everything in the room thrown sideways. I could hear mama's screams, but the room turned, and everything fell against the wall of our cabin. I didn't know what was happening. All I remember after that was a loud cracking sound and the water filling the room. It was freezing." A tear slowly worked its way down her cheek. "It was so cold... and dark. I tried to find my parents, but everything, everything happened so quickly. There were people yelling, and the water was..." She paused, her gaze locked to the short grass below. "I grabbed on to a large piece of wood and held on. I could hear people screaming, and could see the ship burning, but, I couldn't hear mama, or papa. I was alone."

The breeze worked its way between them, the cool air chilling the salted streaks that ran down her cheek as Carlos watched another tear work its way downwards.

Her body shivered lightly as she struggled to remember.

"I have no idea how long I was out there." She slowly brought up her hand to wipe it away. "When I arrived here, I stayed on the beach for two days before I finally made my way through the woods. Then I found the castle." She paused again, her expression turning puzzled. "Now I live here."

Carlos didn't know what to say. He too had lost his parents. He remembered feeling sadness, but he was still too young to truly understand what had happened. It wasn't like hers. His parents hadn't been ripped away from him like that. He hadn't been there when his parents died. He couldn't begin to feel the pain she had felt, or the fear she must have gone through out there alone, floating on a piece of wood in the ocean. He had no words to console her.

"I guess I'm lucky," she continued, breaking the thick silence that had surrounded them. "I could have drowned or been killed when the boat sank."

Carlos let his gaze fall to the steps.

"I see you have met our young bookworm."

Carlos looked up as Isabella flinched and slowly turned.

At the top of the stairs, pants black as night, with pristine white sleeves puffing out of a midnight vest, stood Father. "And how are you liking your new home?"

"Very much sir," Carlos replied, his eyes catching the

flickers of light as the sun glinted off the thin strands of silver that streaked Father's wavy, shoulder length black hair. "Thank you."

"Good," he replied, his eyes slowly moving to Isabella. "And I see you have been busy in the library as well."

Isabella nodded. "I've begun reorganizing the books into category, placing all of them in their own sections."

Father watched as she attempted to hide the sadness from her youthful face.

She paused, her gaze falling to the ruffled, deep crimson bowtie that wrapped tightly around the two protruding collar points below his chin. "It is peaceful. I like it."

Father nodded, looking between the pair before his gaze fell to the trees in the distance. A governed calm brushed past him. He took a deep breath and let his eyes fall back to the pair. "Well," he said, allowing a thin smile to escape. "I can't handle too much sun at this age, so I'll let you get back to your day. I will see you both at dinner."

"Yes sir," Carlos replied, Isabella nodding beside him.

Father threw one last glance at the trees, the darkness hidden just beyond staring back at him. The thin smile on his face faded away.

Carlos turned his gaze to Isabella once Father had

disappeared, the unsettling feeling they both shared holding their words in their throats.

"There's something I can't stop thinking about," Carlos said after a moment, glancing up at the main doors to make sure Father was truly gone. "If there is a monster that hunts in the woods, why doesn't it attack Father when he leads the children to the boats when they leave?"

Isabella glanced at the gate across the grounds for a moment. "There are a lot of things on this island that do not make sense Carlos. If this *is* even truly an island."

A flicker of unease crackled through the air between them.

"Did you see how he looked into the woods?" Carlos asked, taking a deep breath, the soft springtime air filling his lungs as he glanced once more to the twisted gate.

"I'm going to go get ready for dinner," Isabella said after a moment, slowly rising to her feet as she ignored his question; a conversation she was not ready to engage in, not there, not then. The prior had already left a weighted stone in her gut. She needed a moment to collect herself. She could feel the flood of emotions threatening to overtake her, and the thing she prided herself on was her ability to keep those at bay. "I need to wash up."

"Yeah," Carlos said, the feeling still heavy in his chest. "See you at dinner?"

Isabella nodded as she rose to her feet. She forced a thin smile and made her way into the castle.

Carlos stayed on the steps for a moment longer, turning to gaze at the trees beyond. He scanned the towering giants and then rose to make his way inside. He had many questions that he could not form answers to, and somehow knew that Father would not be so quick to provide them. This place was strange—mystical and wondrous, but he couldn't shake the feeling that all of it was not good, that there was something dark, something sinister hiding just beyond the shadows. There was a reason that the beast didn't come near the castle and for a moment, the way that Father had glanced to the woods, Carlos wondered if it was mutual fear that kept it at bay.

THE ROOM

The next few weeks slipped past, time drifting by unnoticed in the unchanging season of the isle. Carlos found himself settled into a routine, basking on the grounds during the day and cleaning the castle floors once the sun had settled beyond the horizon and the halls had fallen silent. He enjoyed working at night, after everyone had returned to their rooms. He lavished in the solitude, and the serenity that the massive hallways imparted to him. He admired the beauty of the castle and found himself frequently transported into worlds only contained in his storybooks with every stroll. There had been times at the orphanage he would sneak out at night, his bare feet slipping along the cold tiles, imagining that Embry was his own private fortress. That was until he had been caught by the groundskeeper. Those walks had immediately ceased after the punishment that had followed. This place was different though, massive and sprawling. The confinement that surrounded him at the orphanage had been traded for the tree line outside. There was an uneasy freedom that lingered around him. He would walk the halls here, not ducking from corner to corner, waiting for the footsteps of the caretaker or groundskeeper, but strolling, stopping to examine the brush strokes on the paintings that hung, or the almost nonexistent chisel marks on the ornate woodwork of the banisters and doorways. He found comfort in his late-night walks and lavished in the peacefulness that it rewarded him. Tonight was no different.

He had waited for the last of the children to make their way to their rooms before going to the kitchen and prepping his mop bucket. He ran hot water and added a small handful of lye shavings. As he stirred the soapy mixture he gazed around the massive space. He imagined the young cooks rushing around the two large, standing islands: food across the pale granite tops. He could see the large copper pots filled with diced vegetables and simmering stews and soups. His mind whirled at the feasts his mind created from the smells that still lingered. There was a sensual aroma that hung in the air, teasing at his taste buds as the water filled the container beneath him. The flash of gruel and stale bread ran past as Embry slunk through the recesses of his memory, breaking his daydream and pulling him back to the bucket at his feet.

He stopped stirring and slowly made his way through the kitchen, admiring the vast, quiet space. He ran his hand across the cold iron stove, inhaling the smell of ash and charcoal and flipped through the pages of the two large cookbooks sitting on top of a table near the black iron oven. He had never cooked before and felt a flash of relief as he turned and made his way to the mop closet. He was happy with the job he had been given. It was as if Father had walked through his mind and picked out the perfect task.

Three hours later he was making his way down a hallway on the third floor. The castle was massive, so he had decided to create a rotating schedule for the spanning hallways. The entryway was first, followed by the halls leading to the dorms and then the one to the library. The second-floor halls were for the following week and the third for the week after. He had just finished the main halls on the third floor, leaving the smaller areas for the following day, and was making his way towards the thin staircase that led up to the fourth floor. Curiosity tugged him closer, serenading him with the excuse that he needed to see how much area there was so that he could better plan how long it would take, should he ever be asked by Father to attend there. Father had specifically said to him never to venture past the third floor, but as many times in his past, rules had a way of fading against his inquisitive nature. He had heard whisperings about what lay above and feared that he might get caught. He had yet to find what punishment would be on the isle, but it was late, and everyone was asleep.

There was a single staircase that led upwards, and the light from his candle disappeared into the blackness halfway up. He steeled himself, mustering as much courage as he could with one deep breath as he held the candle holder into the stairwell. Light cast its shadow upwards, the thin glow confined in the smallest staircase Carlos had seen in the building yet. Everything was so grand in scope compared to the stairwell he was looking up. He felt the walls constricting, closing in, crushing him as he took one step after another. He could feel an air of unease working through him and the darkness seemed to push back against the candle. The hairs on his arms prickled outwards and he could feel the moisture fading in his mouth.

By the time he reached the top step he could feel his heart beating wildly in his chest. He stood there, straining to see down the black hallway as he struggled to rationalize that fear that ebbed through him. He lowered his gaze to the deep crimson carpet that ran along the floor—the color of blood spilt long ago. There were wide columns that stuck out of the walls, reaching up as they curved across the ceiling in a crisscrossed pattern that joined them all together, and just beneath were small insets, old portraits hanging silently in the shadows that wore a thin layer of settled dust across their tops, anxiously waiting to watch any that may venture past.

As he slowly moved down the hall, he could feel a chill growing in the air. He told himself that it was his imagination; that it was his mind playing tricks in the dark, but as his skin pulled tight against his bones, he knew it was more than an illusion. He passed the third pillar when he heard a light fluttering overhead that stopped just behind him. His heart still thumped heavily behind his ribs.

He slowly turned, raising the candle in his trembling hand to illuminate the shadows above. As the edge of light slithered up the wall, he heard another flicker; a tiny shuffle just out of sight and watched as thin trails of dust dropped in translucent streams through the candle's illumination. When the glow finally reached the top ledge, he saw perched atop one of the column edges, the small creature that he and Isabella now referred to as Father's pet. He exhaled sharply, not realizing until that moment that he had been holding his breath tightly behind the screaming urge to run. "It's you, isn't it?" he asked the tiny, scaled creature that gazed down at him from the shadows. "You were at Embry."

The creature flickered its wings and for a moment, a flash of an instant, Carlos swore that its tiny eyes pressed to a squint. It was watching him intently, anticipating his every move. He wasn't supposed to be there, and he could sense that the creature knew it.

"Did you bring me here? And the others?" Carlos continued to speak, a nervous dread slowly filling him as silence responded from the blackness above.

The creature stared at him for a breath, its wings bristling across its back, and then shot a glance through the darkness of the hallway in the direction Carlos had been going. Its gaze fell back to him and then it rose, fluttering its wings for a moment before flying away quickly in the direction of the third floor.

Carlos watched it fly away, a strange amazement working through him. He wondered what the significance of the creature was, and then turned to continue down the hall. Something in the way that the tiny creature had stared at him while he spoke stuck with him as he continued on—it was understanding, in the same manner as a child who is doing something mischievous looks defiantly while being questioned. He could sense that it *knew* what he was saying.

It was another hundred feet before he saw a flicker of light in the dark, a reflection of candlelight casting back at him through the shroud of blackness he was wading through. He paused, slowly lifting the candle to spread the dim light. As he reached the end there was a solitary door. The frame was an ornate sculpture of two wolves standing on their back legs, heads turned upwards in an eternal howl. Above them, was the most beautiful carving Carlos had ever seen; a gold leafed heart, anatomical in all respects, wrapped in a binding of thorned vines.

Carlos stared in amazement, his hand slowly

working the candlelight across the features of the intricate portal in front of him, light flickering off the gold carving above and the ornate knob sitting eyelevel in front of him. His heart began to beat even faster as curiosity pulled his hand towards the etched brass. He could feel the blood pulsing behind his ears as his hand slowly moved out. At that moment, his hand poised mid-air, he felt a presence standing in the darkness behind him.

"You are NEVER, to enter that room!"

Carlos spun, nearly dropping the only illumination to guide him back out.

Standing two feet away, a look of fury twisted across his face, was Father.

Carlos stammered for words as the man's eyes bore into him like an animal stalking its prey.

Father stood silently, unblinking, as Carlos searched desperately for an explanation, his heavy breaths the only sound filling the hall. "You are *never* to come to this floor again," Father said, stepping past him, moving between the outstretched candle and the door as he spoke. "I will not repeat this. Do you understand?"

Carlos nodded as Father's hand moved out to caress the ornate detail spanning the frame. Slowly his fingers traced the vines and moved across the heart as Carlos stood in silence. Father's fingers hovered towards the doorknob and then paused, snapping back quickly as if he expected it to shock or burn him.

"Go, now..." he growled, the tremble in his words sprinkling ice across Carlos's skin.

Carlos started walking backwards down the hall as Father's hunched figure slowly faded away into the black expanse. Then he turned and made his way as quickly as he could without the wind coming off of him extinguishing the flame, back to the third floor and the waiting mop bucket. He blew out the candle and set it on the mantle next to the staircase as he quickly walked to the bucket, grabbing the handle and making his way down the hall.

A short time later he was dumping the dirty contents down the floor drain of the mop closet. His pulse was still racing, and he could feel a bead of sweat lying just beneath his shirt against his back. Then he returned as quickly as he could to the safety of his room. As he undressed and made himself ready for bed his mind replayed the look on Father's face over and over again, each time becoming more and more menacing. There was anger unlike anything he had ever imagined warping his features, a fury that seeded fear deep into his heart. He had felt malice and violence in that piercing gaze, and wondered what it was that had flashed through Father's mind as he was about to touch the handle. Carlos knew that it would be a very long time until he felt comfortable wandering the halls alone and that he would never return to the fourth floor again. Ever.

Above, Father stared at the door. He continued tracing the lines engraved into it, his fingers trembling as the cool wood chilled the tips of his fingers. Even in the darkness he could see the image before him clearly; two beasts rising up to protect the image of life, an image bound and contained. His breathing was heavy in the dark, and he stood silently for a long while, his hand pressed against the anatomical carving. Then a flicker in the hallway pulled his attention away and he stepped back, turning to make his way back down the hall to the third floor. "Yes," he whispered to the invisible shape hovering just behind. "We must keep an eye on that one."

THE LESSON

The next morning Carlos awoke to a light knocking. He rubbed the sleep from his eyes and slowly stood, pulling his pajama bottoms on and making his way to the door.

"Father would like to speak with you."

Carlos was still dazed from being awoken, and before he could ask the younger boy slightly older than himself what it was about, the other turned and made his way quickly down the hall, joining another group that was making the short trek to the dining hall.

The smell of fresh baked bread and crisping bacon wafted past his nose as he slowly stepped back into his room, pulling the door closed behind him. Father's candlelit face flashed in his memory and for an instant he felt the urge to climb back into bed and pretend that the boy had never given him the message. Somehow, he got the feeling that Father would know otherwise, so he slowly dressed and made his way down the hall. As he passed the dining hall, he could see the other children sitting at their tables, laughing and eating, the morning fog quickly dissipating from the room as bellies slowly became full and the room became louder. He didn't see Isabella, either she had skipped breakfast and headed straight to the library, or she'd already eaten and made her way to the yard to read. She was always one of the first ones up in the morning. He would joke about how she should have been one of the bakers instead. "I burn toast," she would reply with a laugh. "I'm not exactly sure the others would like to wake up to burnt rolls every morning."

The pleasantries quickly faded away as he made his way past the foyer and down the hall that led to Father's chambers. As he approached his footsteps slowed and he felt his stomach beginning to knot nervously. Isabella and the smells of breakfast had dissipated from his thoughts altogether.

He paused at the door before lightly knocking.

"Please," he heard, Father's voice drifting through the wood, a calm tone carrying the words softly to his ears. "Enter."

Carlos turned the knob and slowly pushed the door open, making his way inside, the knot gently tightening as he stepped into the large room.

As he closed the door behind him, Father was sitting in his chair at the end, the roaring face of violence now gone, replaced with the caring gaze that Carlos had met weeks before.

"Please," Father said, extending his hand. "Come forward."

Carlos slowly stepped towards him, struggling to ignore the feeling that screamed for him to turn and run, to make for the safety of the exit.

"Allow me to begin with an apology," Father said as Carlos approached. "I did not mean to startle you last evening."

Carlos stared quietly, his gaze taking in the black vest and white ruffles beneath it, avoiding the man's gaze as long as possible.

"I just need you to understand," he continued. "There is only one room in my home that I hold sacred; one place where none may enter. Everywhere else in this castle is open, to be shared, and enjoyed by those of you that have become part of this family." He paused as seriousness visited his features for a moment. "But as you have the sanctity of your own space here, that room is held private to you. So, I trust that you can understand, when I find someone attempting to enter the one place that is held dear to me, that such as I'm sure you would, I feel as though my hospitality is being... *pressed*."

Carlos held his gaze to the floor beneath the chair.

Father studied the young boy. He could see that he was afraid of him, afraid of being punished. It was a look he had grown quite accustomed to over the years. "I mean no harm, nor do I mean to instill fear," Father continued, the calm in his voice finally beginning to penetrate the wall Carlos had built on his way to his quarters. "But without rules, there would be no order, and lack of order bequeaths chaos. Chaos is what has driven all of you to this island, what has brought you all to *me*. It is chaos that destroyed your lives, killed those that you loved and gave those around you the ability to hate and cause you harm."

A squint gently tugged at the edge of Carlos's eyes. He had not told Father about his parent's death, nor had he told him about his treatment at the orphanage. An unseen chill quietly brushed through the room.

Father continued to study him, his gaze moving across every line on his face. "I have very few rules here," he continued, sternness edging closer into his words. "Do not harm those that are your family, do not enter the woods beyond the grounds, complete the tasks that help us live in a functioning home, and never, ever, attempt to enter that room." He paused, his gaze locked to him. "Do you understand these rules my son?"

Carlos nodded, his gaze moving to the floor for a moment.

"This is a place for those like yourself to escape to, a place that the homeless could call home, a place where those without family, could find and become one. These walls are open to those that have been cast away, that the outside world, humanity, no longer care about."

"Why are there only children here?" Carlos asked, blurting the question that had been haunting him since his arrival. "Where are the grownups?" He looked up to meet Father's gaze. "Why are there no adults here?"

Father stayed quiet for a moment, studying Carlos who had brought his hands together nervously in front of him. He had heard this question before. "Am I not an adult?" he responded with a slight grin.

"Yes," Carlos stammered. "But I mean, others."

Father took a deep breath, exhaling slowly before responding. "Those that are grown, can no longer be saved," Father replied softly. "They have already become set in their ways, destroyed by an uncivilized society. You see, humanity by its nature, is designed to destroy itself. It is inherent in each of... us, to live in greed and selfish abandon. To those that grow older, the magic of this place is lost, and they always seek to explore beyond. It is simply not safe. I alone remain, because of my duty, and charge, to keep watch over this island, and those that are brought here."

We were brought here..., Carlos thought silently as he watched Father's lips twitch for the briefest moment.

Father stared for a moment longer, taking a deep breath and exhaling loudly. The boy before him was unmoved by his explanation, and he could see that the fires of curiosity were only stoked. "You *can* change, and it is here that I give you that opportunity. It is within these walls that I hope each and every one of you finds your true capacity for humanity." Father paused, his eyes flickering as they peered down at Carlos. "Is the question that you mean to ask, where are the children that have grown up here?"

Carlos stayed quiet.

"And why are they no longer living among us?"

He wanted to run.

Father continued to study him before continuing, picking carefully his words to satiate the youth who nodded once in reply. "This island has been here for a very long time my son, far longer than I, and will be here far longer after *we* are all gone. I have seen countless come and go, and helped more than I can count while they were here and led them to the fates that await them beyond the safety of these grounds."

Carlos's toes twitched in his shoes as anxiety pressed into him.

Father rubbed the solid arm of the chair he sat in, his hand working around the wolf's head that protruded from the end of each. The wood was cool to the touch, comforting. "The world beyond this island is a very harsh place, and those that need most desperately to escape, always find their way here. But I cannot offer protection forever you see. Once those that are our family feel that they are ready to return to the world in which they came from, and feel that they no longer need our protection, then, they are free to go, and I offer them the freedom to return to that place." He paused, gazing out the window for a moment. "Yes, I am always sad to see them go, but no one stays forever. It is I alone, who bears that burden, and gift—a price that must be paid." His eyes moved back and locked to Carlos. "Now," he said, a smile creeping its way across his jaw. "I'm sure you would like to get on with enjoying your day. You are young, go, enjoy it. It is fleeting, and we must savor every moment. It is childhood that *feeds* our adulthood after all."

Carlos nodded, then turned to make his way towards the exit, struggling against the screaming desire to run.

Father watched him turn, making his way towards the door as quickly as he could without breaking into a sprint. He waited until he was nearly at his escape.

"Carlos," he said as the boy reached for the door handle. "Mind the rules of this house, and no harm will befall you."

Carlos paused, then turned the knob and made his way back into the hall.

As he walked towards the dining hall he felt his stomach churn. His appetite had been left in that room this morning and he wanted nothing more than to escape the closing walls and feel the fresh spring air on his skin. He turned to the stairs in the foyer and took them three at a time, releasing his legs to run across the smooth marble until grass cushioned the falls of his feet. He didn't stop. He ran until he had made it all the way to the back of the estate. By the time he reached the fountain his lungs were burning, and his legs felt like they were going to fall out from under him.

As he approached the marble structure, he let the weight on his legs give out and dropped in front of it, sliding his back against the cool stone as he folded his arms across his legs, his knees to his chest. Carlos felt fear envelope him. Not like the panic he had felt when the other boys chased him down the orphanage hall, or the feeling he felt when the headmaster would reach for her leather strap. He felt real fear, the kind that stabbed like a dagger into your chest and slowly twisted. The kind that pulled your skintight against your skeleton and parched the liquid from your throat, the kind that left you trembling on a warm day.

For the next hour he sat under the lip of the fountain, his gaze locked to the grass that extended to the trees two hundred yards away. It wouldn't be until he lay down that night that the feeling would finally begin to separate from him, and Father's voice would fade from his ears.

SUSPICION

The next day Carlos made his way through the mansion. The morning sun filled the hallways with colorful, dancing light as it blazed through the stained glass above. This morning, however, he walked completely unaware of the beauty of the castle's construction that had struck him every day prior. His steps were slow, his head down and clouded in thought. The boy that had crept unseen through the orphanage had returned. He had skipped breakfast, the prior night and morning's conversation still holding his appetite at bay. It wasn't until the familiar smell of aged parchment and leather filled his nose that he realized he had been walking straight towards the library.

He made his way in, stopping in the middle to look around. The room was empty. "Isabella?" he called out, the rows of books that reached to the ceiling muffling any echo that should have answered back.

"Up here," came the light reply from the second floor a moment later.

Isabella had been organizing a shelf on the upper tier, removing the books carefully, dusting them and placing them back in alphabetical order. She had been there since breakfast.

Carlos felt a gentle warmth move to his lips as he took a deep breath, exhaling the pressure that had been building inside him.

He moved to the stairs that led up, making his way around the circle to where his friend stood, two stacks of books at her feet. Her hair was tied up and he could see a small bead of sweat on her brow as he approached. "I missed you at breakfast," she said, turning with a smile as he approached.

"I wasn't feeling too well," he replied.

"I'm sorry. Is everything all right?"

Carlos nodded.

"Good," she replied with another grin. "Then would you mind helping me?" She extended her arms, handing Carlos a stack of books that looked precariously close to dropping. "Thank you. I guess I got a little carried away."

Carlos smiled faintly; his mind still held by Father's enraged face.

"If I can get these finished today, I'll be able to move onto the next section in the morning." She paused, wiping the moisture from her face away with her sleeve. "I may have time to finish the book I'm in the middle of also." She stared at Carlos for a moment, realizing that his face was sullen, and the usual glow of intrigue was gone, replaced with a mask of heavy contemplation. "What's wrong?"

Carlos stared at the books in front of him for a moment before speaking. "Have you ever seen Father angry?"

Isabella looked at him curiously for a moment before responding, a smile moving across her lips. "No." She paused again; her brow furrowed. "What did you do Carlos?"

Carlos set the books down on the table and recounted the night before, telling her how he had approached the fourth-floor room, and how Father had almost appeared out of nowhere. Then he told her of the small creature and how he felt it had been watching him, like it had told on him.

"Wait…" Isabella exclaimed, her gaze moving quickly around the library. "You think the creature *told* on you...?"

"One moment it was there, and the next, Father appeared… And when I spoke to it, I swear, I don't know how to explain it, but I could feel that it knew what I was saying—it understood me."

Isabella took a deep breath, staring at him for a moment as if studying him before setting two of the three books she still held in her hands on the floor near one of the shelves. Her eyes again scanned the room, glancing quickly to the top of the bookshelves before continuing. "There's something I need to tell you," she said, her gaze moving back to him as her voice lowered. "Not here."

Carlos stared at her for a moment. The puzzled smile she wore was now gone.

She nodded towards the stairs and turned to make her way out of the library. Silently they made their way down the hallway and towards the foyer. Isabella didn't turn to look at Carlos as he followed quietly behind. He could sense that there was something she had been meaning to say for quite some time—the feeling of the proverbial elephant slowly creeping into the room. It wasn't until they were making their way around the castle that she looked back at him.

"Over here," she said, moving out into the grounds.

Carlos followed her to the middle of the grass that spanned to the forest. For a moment she stood, glancing around before taking a seat in the grass and opening the book in front of them.

Carlos stood there for a moment. He glanced around before sitting himself, his friend's sudden change of demeanor beginning to wear into him. Before he could speak, she began. "I saw Father's pet before I even arrived here. It was there before my family left on the boat, and again right before the boat sank. I swear I saw that *thing*, standing in the window of our cabin."

He glanced down for a moment, the vision of the creature on the log flashing vividly. "Are you sure?" he asked, the image of the strange sprite sitting atop the log at the orphanage flashing past.

"I don't think something like that is easily imagined," she replied. "Yes. I'm sure."

"What do you think it is?" Carlos asked after a moment.

Isabella shrugged. "I don't know, but..." she said after a moment. "When did *you* first see it?"

"At the orphanage," he replied, the image of the small creature staring up at him flashing into his mind. "At the orphanage. It was there right before I escaped. It was almost like it was showing me the path I used when I escaped. The one that led me to the boat that brought me here. He paused, remembering the moment that the creature had flown into the trees and down the trail he had followed that had led to the boat. "Yeah. If I had not seen it, I don't think I would have followed that path. I never would have ended up here..."

The pair stayed quiet, both pondering the unspoken coincidence of the small creature appearing right before they appeared on the island as they stared at each other.

Isabella felt a ripple slowly creep across her skin. "So, both of us saw it right before we landed on this island," she said, pondering quietly for a moment. "We're not the first to say that."

"Others too?" Carlos asked.

"I've heard two others tell a similar story," she continued. "One boy said his house burnt down in the middle of the night and he was the only one to escape. He ran in fear of being blamed and stowed away on a ship. Then, like myself, something happened, and the ship sunk. He woke up here a few days later. He also followed the strange creature, which led him to the docks. That's how he ended up here."

Carlos felt the skin beneath his shirt slowly ripple as it tightened.

"The other boy said his family was on holiday when a storm hit the island his family was on. The same thing. He saw the creature right before it happened, and then ended up here..."

"You don't think it caused the storms do you...? Carlos asked.

"No, I wouldn't go that far, but it's more than coincidence that in all the stories, our families are killed, we are swept out to sea, and then we arrive here..."

Carlos stared at her for a moment, Father's words filling back into his ears.

"Father told me yesterday when he called me to his office, that we were *brought* here, that none of us has landed here by accident.

Isabella stared at him for a moment, worry flooding across her face. "Then... It, brought us here?"

"I don't know," Carlos replied quietly. "That was all he said. We were brought."

Isabella stared quietly, thoughts of her family flooding into her, accompanied by the small creature that watched the island. Sadness slowly morphed into disgust, and disgust to anger. "Did they *kill* my parents?"

Carlos startled. "Who? Father and that creature? No... I mean. I don't think so." Carlos struggled to find words, or rationale in the entire situation. "My family died long before I ever saw it.

"But still. It's the same story. You saw it watching you, and now you're here...

Carlos felt the prickling along his arms return.

"It can't be coincidence that it was there every time, with each of us."

There was spite lacing Isabella's words as she spoke, a suspicious tone hiding just behind.

She paused, her gaze moving to the castle for a moment. Overhead the breeze brush slowly past, coriander and jasmine floating on the air. From the moment she had arrived, there had been something sinister hiding just beyond the shadows, watching them as they went unnoticing about their days. It was a feeling that she knew must be shared and unspoken by every one of them.

"I always have the feeling that it's watching us, the other children don't seem to notice it, but I always see it hovering, just out of view as if listening to our conversations." She paused again, a whisper moving through her voice. "And the monster that lives in the woods...? And Father, who almost never leaves his room and looks as if he's in pain when he goes outside..." She stared at him for a moment. "Carlos... Something's not right about this place."

Across the yard a group of children erupted into laughter, a giant ball bouncing between them. Isabella flinched, her eyes flashing in the direction of the sound for a moment.

"Look around... A paradise for children with endless food and treats, no supervision and not even so much as a bedtime...?"

Carlos stayed quiet. He had been feeling it as well, from the moment he arrived; the unsettling feeling that things weren't as they seemed. It had been gnawing at him since the moment he had stepped out of the boat, and oddly, it was relieving that he was not the only one who felt it, but more so, at the same time, that much more unnerving.

"I just think that we need to be careful," Isabella said after a moment. "And I don't think we should have this conversation with anyone else either... Just in case."

Carlos nodded. "I don't trust Father," he said, glancing at the grass as he spoke. "There's something about him that scares me."

Isabella stared at him for a moment before her gaze fell to the book in her hands. "Me too."

The pair sat in silence for the next few minutes, neither knowing what to say as the castle loomed over them silently a short distance away.

Their conversation had been carried away by the

wind.

"I'm gonna get back to the library," Isabella said after a moment, folding the book and standing up.

She turned to walk away, stopping after a few steps to turn around. "We need to be careful here."

Carlos nodded as she turned back around and walked towards the entrance. He felt a mixture of warmth and prickling cold forming around him, like wearing a warm jacket on a snowy night. He was glad to finally have a friend, but she was also right. Something was strange about the island. And now that he felt it, he couldn't push the feeling away.

For the next three days he walked the grounds and the halls, watching the other children run carefree, doing their chores and stuffing themselves fat. No one seemed to care, or even put a flicker of question into where they were or how they had gotten there. To them it was paradise, a world away from the torment and anxiety they had been surrounded in during their lives before. Everyone was happy and even he found it hard to keep up the suspicion as the days crept by.

CURIOSITY

Another two days had fallen past, yet the conversation that had left him on edge still clung lightly to the back of his mind. Things had seemingly returned to normal, all sense of foreboding and conspiracy fading into a haze of blue skies and full stomachs. Even Isabella seemed to have returned to her normal routine of eating and reclusing to the library to surround herself with endless tomes until late afternoon, where they would meet up and chat on the grass near the fountain. Today, however, she had decided to stay late to finish up the section she had been working on. Her mind was wrapped in the numbers and bindings that surrounded her, carefully pulling different books from the shelves and glancing through them in order to find where they would be best situated.

She had placed an older book written completely in Latin on a small stack that was meant to go into her foreign language section when she not so much as heard but felt a presence standing behind her.

She slowly turned around to see Father standing just inside the doorway, his gaze moving around the room slowly. He was taking in every binding, every row with careful precision, noting every change she had made without a blink of his eye. When he had scanned all the way to the second floor he turned his gaze upon her.

Isabella stayed quiet, assuming there was a reason for his visit, as he had never once stepped foot into the library since her arrival. She only hoped it wasn't pertaining to her and Carlos's conversation the days prior.

"I see you have been making great strides," he said after an awkwardly long pause.

She smiled, glancing around quickly. One long curl of hair had fallen down in front, and she pushed it back behind her ear. "I still have a long way to go." She paused, a thought striking her like a hot iron. "Will we ever get more books? I worry what I'm going to do when everything is organized and there's nothing more to be done."

Father stared at her for a moment, his gaze piercing deeply into her. "I will see to it that arrangements are made when we reach that moment," he replied. "But for now, there is still plenty of work to be done around the castle."

Isabella nodded. The thought stuck with her. She assumed that in a worst-case scenario she could simply begin rearranging in a different order. At least the books would stay dusted.

Father looked at her for another moment, his brow furrowing together slightly. "Are you happy here?" he asked, his question flat and cold.

She stared at him for a moment. She could feel that

he knew something, but it was well hidden behind the mask of false worry. "Why do you ask?" she replied, curiosity puncturing the question.

"I happened to hear from one or two of the other children that you may have seemed troubled these past few days. I was simply concerned."

A squint flashed through her eyes. She hated it when people intruded in her affairs. This was among the reasons she kept mainly to herself. She could feel heat rising in her face, and instantly her cheeks became flush. "Well maybe these, other children, should learn to mind their own business and not go telling others how it is that they *assume* it is, that I may, or may not feel."

Father stood silent, a stone statue peering emotionless at her.

"I find it rather rude that they would find themselves telling you how it is that I feel, and not coming directly to me and asking first. But for their information, I'm doing just fine. I spend my time here so that I don't have to be part of that juvenile play. I enjoy my company here, and that that I keep outside. What I do is my own affair, as is how I feel."

The more she spoke, the angrier she could feel herself becoming. It wasn't Father's fault, and for a brief moment she almost felt sorry for her outburst, but that faded quickly when she realized that he could have simply ignored it all together.

Father inhaled sharply, the wrinkle across his forehead disappearing as he allowed himself to relax. He could hear the thin growl behind a veil of darkness whispering. He admired her defiance. It reminded him of the youth he had once been, long ago. He gazed upon her, her lips pursed together, the curl that had again escaped the clutches of her ear, the suspicious gaze that she stared back with. No one had approached him. Nothing had been said of her. He simply used youth's pension for tattling and gossip as a means to infiltrate the true feelings of his wards. For a moment, a thin smile tugged at his lips as he pondered the outcome of any who may find themselves standing opposite her good side. He had just seen a glimmer of what lay behind the calm, book-shrouded demeanor that she carried about her. Inside him, something twisted, contorting to get a better view. "I'll be sure to reiterate your message should any of the others find themselves in the mood of interfering in your affairs," he said, breaking his gaze to take in the disarray that was fading substantially. Then he turned and made his way back out, disappearing into the hallway.

Isabella stood there for a moment, her emotions beginning to slowly simmer to a calm. His words had angered her. Not so much at the thought of other children prying into her affairs, but the fact that a little bit of the isolation she enjoyed had now been tarnished.

She turned and made her way to the small alcove set aside for herself on the second floor and pulled out the book she was working her way through. She opened the flap to her mark and took a deep breath, exhaling as she allowed her gaze to fall to the space that had just been occupied by Father.

A HORROR FOUND

Outside, Carlos found himself wandering the edge of the woods surrounding the estate grounds. He had taken this to be his daily routine, finding a soothing tranquility in it. He enjoyed the sounds of the woods; distant bird songs and cricket chirps, mixed with the sounds of children laughing and chatting near the castle. That was a feeling that had yet to fade. Each day the sprawling estate was becoming more and more his home, the frightened memory of Father's face and unanswered questions fading away more and more with each meal eaten and long afternoons spent basking in the sun. There was a type of magic on the isle, an ebbing forgetfulness that seemed to soothe its way closer and closer with each passing day.

He had made his way to the back, halfway between the castle and the fountain that he spent countless hours lying upon, reading and daydreaming. He was swinging a stick in the air, pretending to be one of the swordfighters from the Alexandre Dumas books that Isabella had forced him to read; a rare copy printed in English, when something caught his eye. A short distance ahead a small animal sat in the grass. He stopped, the stick still held in his grasp lowering to his side as he watched the squirrel slowly chewing on a fruit that had fallen from a nearby tree. It sat there for a moment staring back at him and then turned, darting quickly into the trees.

Carlos made his way to where the squirrel had been and noticed what appeared to be a small opening behind the dense shrub. He set down his sword and moved the brush aside. Just behind was a large, hollow log. It stretched into the woods some ten feet, and he could see what appeared to be a small path at the other end.

He slowly let the brush fall back into place, turning to look around. The grounds were empty and as far as he could see, he was the only one on this side of the castle. He pushed the brush aside easily and made his way through the hollowed trunk. Moments later he was standing at the other side, a thick wall of foliage blocking the castle from view. He smiled inwardly, a sense of adventure filling him as he turned to the path leading deeper into the trees. As he began to step forward Father's words fell back into his ears. *Never go into the woods. There is a monster that feeds upon children.* He paused, his feet holding in place for a moment before curiosity won the battle and he continued forward. The path had been used before, and that meant it had to lead somewhere.

The woods that surrounded him were thick, giant trees reaching up to meet in a massive canopy that spanned as far as he could see. Tall brush and flowers layered the ground between them, and the smell of moist bark and peat hung heavy in the air. He walked along the path for the next hour, the sounds of the forest filling his ears and a cool breeze brushing his skin as it slowly moved past. He followed the tiny trail, taking notice that no one had walked along it in a very long time. Grass grew from the trampled earth in thick patches and occasionally the trail would appear to disappear altogether. The nervous ping brought on by the looming fear of the monster had dissipated as the fantasy world around him quietly pulled him deeper inwards. Occasionally he would stop and look back to make sure the path was still there and that he had not somehow turned off of it. He knew what the cost of getting lost could be, the image of emerald eyes still lingering behind his thoughts.

An hour later he crossed a small stream, stopping for a moment to listen to the soft sound of water bubbling lightly past. He stood at the creek side for a moment, watching a swarm of insects hovering above, when he realized that he had not brought food or water with him on the unexpected journey, and that for the first time since entering the woods that his mouth was dry, and he was beginning to feel thirst scratch at his throat. As he knelt down and let the water fill his hand he paused, a strange smell wafting past his nose, pungent and foul, like an animal left out in the sun too long after death. He looked up and saw that a short distance deeper into the trees was what appeared to be a massive clearing. He could see from where he was at, that an area roughly a hundred feet across looked as if it stood empty. Nothing was there, just open space. He raised his hand to his mouth and slowly drank, his eyes locked to the empty space, the sour smell brushing past him again in a pungent breeze. Slowly he stood, wiping his hands dry on his pants and took his first steps towards the clearing.

As he got closer the odor became stronger, and it was a few feet later that he brought his shirt up over his nose and found himself holding his breath. He drew nearer to the open space and realized that it wasn't a clearing, but a massive hole in the ground, like the earth had collapsed and swallowed a giant piece of the forest with it. He felt a cold nervousness worming its way into him as he took each step closer to the hidden horror. He moved cautiously, with a grasping reluctance as he edged closer to the line of trees that bordered the pit. When he reached the edge he froze, a cold nausea filling his gut as the skin around his small frame rose in a sea of gooseflesh. Ten feet down and spread the entire way across were scattered bones and corpses well into rot. He felt his skin pull back as a wave of panic rushed through him, his eyes open wide, locked to the scene before him. His stomach lurched and he turned his head to the side, vomiting heavily into the soil. Before him was unfathomable death, carnage his mind couldn't have created in even its worst nightmares. Rising up to coalesce in a pungent cloud was old death and decay.

When the retching subsided and he was able to pull his gaze from the wet puddle at his feet, he lifted his gaze and turned back to the horror beneath. He stood there, his feet rooted to the earth beneath, body shaking as his gaze held locked to the gruesome cavity until the sound of a branch snapping in the woods beyond ripped him from the invisible binds he was held by.

Carlos startled, his gaze flashing in the direction of the sound, quickly wiping the spittle from his lips. It was one breath before he turned and bolted back in the direction of the path. When he found the trail, he continued to run as fast as he could, the feeling of a giant beast reaching with razor claws at his back, pushing him to continue even as his legs threatened to give out beneath him and his lungs begged him to stop. He ran until his body was ready to collapse, and when he thought he would be able to go no further, saw the log at the edge of the woods. He dropped to his knees and crawled as fast as he could through the tiny tunnel, not pausing as he shoved the bush aside and scrambled onto the castle grounds where he collapsed, his breath coming in rapid heaves. His throat was dry, the muscles in his legs on fire and his mind was racing with the images that now burned just behind his eyes. He lay there in the grass for the next few minutes, his gaze locked to the blue sky above as the sounds of the woods slowly faded back in and the beating of his heartbeat grew distant in his ears. He struggled to grasp what he had just seen. Father had been right. There was a monster that stalked the woods and fed upon children. He *had* seen the creature from his window that night. There was something evil hidden amongst the trees. He had to warn the others. He had to tell Isabella. Everything they had been told was true. Every fear they had was real.

He stood and started making his way back towards the castle, his hands still shaking as he walked. His back and chest were covered in sweat and his shirt was saturated from running through the woods. He walked tiredly towards the main entrance, his legs struggling to keep him up as they shook beneath him. As he passed the fountain and made his way to the front he looked up. Just above the first floor, sitting on a ledge below the second-floor windows was the small winged creature; Father's pet. He gazed up at it for a minute, watching as it stared down at him. Though the lizard-like face was nearly void of expression, he could almost sense the suspicion coming from it. He stared at it for a moment before it flittered its wings and rose, flying upwards and over the castle out of view. Carlos continued around, making his way up the stairs and down the hall towards the library. As he approached his steps slowed. He was at ends with himself. On one hand, he felt he needed to tell his friend what he had seen, it was his obligation. She needed to know, had a right to, but at the same time, he didn't want to be the one responsible for ruining all of this for her. She was happy. Her family was gone, and here, at least she had a home, and friends. She didn't have to worry. Father had said, that as long as they didn't venture into the woods they would be unharmed. But he had wandered, and he had seen the death. Now all that was different. Now the fairy tale had been twisted.

He stopped, standing just feet from the library entrance. He would tell her, but just not yet. Everyone knew the story of the monster roaming the woods. Her knowing the truth behind the tales would offer no comfort. It would do none of them any good, and he didn't wish to give his only friend a reason to want to leave. He knew it was selfish, but this was the first time in his life he had ever held friendship, and he was clinging desperately to it. He couldn't lose it.

"What are you doing?"

Carlos snapped his gaze up from the floor, startled to see Isabella standing in front of him, inspecting him up and down with a mild look of disgust. "You're filthy... and sweaty..."

"Uh," Carlos stammered. "Uh... yeah... I was uh... I was cleaning out the fountain. I... I thought it would be nice to get it working."

Isabella smiled, her disgust slowly turning to amusement. "You know… You're a really bad liar…" Isabella smiled with a small shake of her head and then walked past him, tapping him on the arm as she did. "Come on…"

The pair walked a short way down the hall when she spoke up again, breaking the awkward silence. "You know you can tell me anything right?" she asked from behind.

Carlos slowed, letting her walk beside him.

"I'm not stupid. You wouldn't work up a sweat like that and get covered in scratches from cleaning the fountain…"

Carlos nodded.

Isabella shook her head with a scoff. "Boys…" She turned and made her way down the hall leaving him standing there.

He watched her walk away and turned to make his way towards his room. As he did, he saw the creature hovering at the top of the stairs leading to Father's room. He paused, staring at it as it fluttered for a second and then turned to dart down the hall. Carlos went to his room and undressed, setting himself a bath and soaking until it was time to go to dinner. He struggled to get the image of the pit out of his head but no matter how tightly he closed his eyes, the small bones and rotting corpses haunted his mind. Sitting alone in his room, the smell continued to waft past on phantom air.

A Request for Leave

Days passed. The unchanging sky overhead sitting wrapped in a blanket of unchanging blue. Carlos was sitting at the base of the main stairs, a waning ball of sweet bread held loosely in his hand as he chatted with two other children that had made their way out. The scene in the woods still sat fresh with him, and every conversation he had was laced with the faces of death.

"That's not what I heard," a younger girl with long black hair the color of a raven's wing said. "She told me that she wasn't sure her parents were dead and wanted to go back to see for herself."

"But you can't just leave and then return," a slightly older boy replied. "Father has told us that once we leave, that we can no longer come back to the isle."

"No," the other replied. "He said we're always welcome back, just none of the others ever return."

Carlos sat listening to the pair's conversation. He had seen the children that would never return. The pair was wrong. They never left. "Who is going to leave?" he asked, fearing that another child was to be led through the woods and possibly fall prey to the monster.

The girl looked at him and wrinkled her face, responding as if puzzled how it was that he could be completely oblivious to the rumor that seemingly everyone knew of. "Marianna..."

"Oh," Carlos replied, feigning his knowledge of what child the name was attached to.

"Father has given his ok to leave, and later today we'll have her parting ceremony," the boy added. There was a cold excitement in his words.

"Parting ceremony?" Carlos asked, slightly confused about what leaving the island fully entailed.

The pair exchanged a quick glance. "He's the new boy," the girl whispered.

"Oh," the older boy replied with a smile. "Well, if one of us decides to leave; though for the life of me, I still can't understand why anyone would want to, but when they do, we celebrate their time here with us, and the friendship that we have made and will miss when they are gone. We all gather in the banquet hall for a special feast, and Father gives his farewell speech. Then we all gather to say our goodbyes and Father leads them to the boat that will take them back to wherever it was that they came here from."

Embry Estate flashed through Carlos's mind, the wicked face of the headmaster snarling at him through the invisible haze.

"Do they have to go back to where they came from or can they go somewhere else?" he asked, apprehension building up behind his words.

"No," the boy replied. "As long as Father knows where to send the boat, you can go there. New York,

London, Dublin... Wherever you want."

The feeling dissipated on a slow, unseen breath that Carlos had been subconsciously holding.

"You'll see," the boy said. "Her parting ceremony is tonight." The boy paused, smiling at the girl. "Just make sure you have an empty stomach. There're always the most amazing treats. It's one of the times other than Christmas that Father shares recipes from his personal book."

Carlos looked at him puzzled and the girl sitting down caught it quickly.

"Boris is one of the cooks here," she said, a sense of pride in her words.

"Oh," Carlos replied, turning his attention to the boy. "The food is amazing, thank you."

The boy smiled back. "But, with that being said, I should be going. The others have probably already begun." The boy turned to the girl, nodding with a smile.

As he turned to make his way back into the mansion he nearly ran full force into Isabella who was making her way down the stairs behind him with a book in one hand and a perfectly red apple in the other.

"Goodness," he said as he dodged quickly to the side to avoid piling into her. "You scared me."

Isabella stood there, her eyebrows raised, staring at the boy who blushed sheepishly and then hurried past her.

"Hey," Carlos said as she made her way down the three stairs between them.

"What was that about?" she asked, glancing over her shoulder to where the boy had disappeared to.

"Something about a parting ceremony...?" Carlos replied, his gaze falling to the mansion door as well. "That was one of the cooks; Boris."

"Oh," Isabella replied, a slight irritation worn on her face. "And the girl?"

"Oh!" Carlos said, turning around to the empty space where the girl had been standing. "Where'd she go?"

"It's not important. Look, I'm not feeling so well," she said, a tone of sadness in her words. "I'm gonna sit in the yard for a while."

"Would you like some company?" Carlos asked, worry edging into him.

"I think I have all the company I need," she said, a smile hinting at her lips as her hands closed tighter on the book she held. "Thank you though."

"Ok," Carlos replied, watching as she started down the stairs. "See you at the ceremony?"

Isabella nodded, already reaching the grass at the bottom.

Carlos took a deep breath, watching as his friend made her way out into the spanning grounds, then turned and made his way back inside.

As he walked the halls, he watched as four other children ran past laughing and chasing each other. The thought of leaving sat heavy in his mind. He had no desire to himself, but at the same time wondered, if he was ready one day, would he be able to go, and where could his options be. He approached the stairs leading to the second floor, the questions still raging in his mind, and it wasn't until he was standing in front of the door to Father's chambers that he realized what he was doing. He reached his hand out and tapped lightly against the door. A moment later he heard Father's soft reply filter through the thick wood. "You may enter."

Carlos pushed the door open, walking into the long room. As the door closed behind him, he saw Father sitting in his chair at the opposite end. He looked up as Carlos began making his way through the room, setting a book he had been reading down on the arm of the massive seat and greeting him as he approached.

Father watched him make his way across the room. The child stepping towards him seemed to always carry an air of worry about him, his shoulders almost always hunched as if protecting him from an impending blow.

"Hello Carlos," he said, a smile moving across his face. "Is everything ok?"

"Yes Father," Carlos replied, still struggling to formulate how to begin the conversation. "Thank you."

"And what brings you to me today?"

Carlos shifted uneasily, his hands moving together in front of him. He realized his palms were moist and he had become extremely uncomfortable; a feeling that grew every time he remembered Father's angered scowl. He now regretted knocking. "I wondered if I might ask a question."

Father stared at Carlos for a moment, studying him carefully before responding, his smile growing wider. "Of course, my son, please."

Carlos took a deep breath, exhaling slowly as he wiped his palms against his pants. "If one day, I wished to leave, to try and start a new life somewhere else, is that…. Is that possible? Could I do that?" His words were weak, and the last part of his sentence was delivered in a fearful stammer of words.

Father tensed in his chair, his eyes flashing to a squint for a fleeting moment before he leaned back in his chair. "Well Carlos. As I would be truly sad to see another child leave, it would only do to accommodate your request." He paused, the smile fading. "You would be allowed to leave, though I would strongly suggest that you put a fair amount of thought into your decision."

Carlos glanced at the floor for a moment before raising his eyes to meet Father's again.

"It is still as I told you before my child. No one is captive on this island; save for myself. You are *all* free to leave on your own volition. And though it saddens me greatly every time, I would make sure you were taken to wherever it was you wished to go."

Father studied him for another moment, his head moving to the side slightly in a subtle suspicious manner.

"I'm sorry, but there's something that I can't stop thinking about," Carlos blurted, his eyes falling to the steps. "If there's a monster in the woods, how is it that you can lead the children to the boats and make your way back without being killed?"

Father stared silently, the unseen shape behind his mind slowly pulling itself awake at the question. Deep behind his eyes there was an unheard growl. "You see Carlos," Father began in his practiced calm. "I have been here a very long time. I provide for the island, and in turn, the island provides for me—for us. I know when it is safe to travel the woods, and when it is not. Those that accompany me have nothing to fear, save for the world beyond these grounds." Father paused, a shiver running through him. "You aren't thinking of leaving us already, are you?"

Carlos looked up at him, not realizing his gaze was still on the floor at his feet. "No!" he replied quickly. "It's just... I heard that a girl was leaving today, to try and find her parents. I just wanted to know that if one day I wanted to leave, to start a new life, somewhere else, that I could. That was all. I'm not thinking of leaving."

Father eased a bit. "Yes. Marianna will be leaving us

today." He paused, his gaze moving to one of the stained-glass windows above. "As I said before, it is always sad," he said, his gaze held to the red and orange glass. "Losing another child."

His gaze moved back to Carlos.

"But I suppose that is the nature of youth; to be ever seeking, bound by curiosity with no end. I suppose this island can only offer so much before the routine of it devours them and they wish only to seek change, to metamorphose into an adult and become like those that were the cause of their arrival here." Father paused. "This is one of the things that will never change."

Carlos began to feel awkward. He had only wished to ask his question and then leave, and so, found himself fidgeting as Father became lost in his verbal thoughts.

"I apologize," Father said, sensing his anticipation. "I tend to ramble sometimes. Yes. If the day comes that you wish to leave us, you must but tell me, and I will ensure you get to your desired destination."

Carlos nodded, his gaze flashing to the floor again.

"Was that the extent of your visit Carlos?" Father said, extending his hand to the door.

"Yes," he replied, his legs already yearning for him to turn.

"Then enjoy the rest of your day, and I will see you at dinner."

"Thank you," Carlos replied, slowly turning to make

his way out.

"And Carlos."

"Yes?" he said, stopping in his tracks to turn his gaze back to the chair.

"Remember. The woods beyond are not safe without my accompaniment. They are not to be ventured into. Harm *will* befall you if you do."

Carlos nodded, a cold chill running through him. He knew… Instantly he knew that the creature had seen him clambering back out of the log. A slew of questions battered him as he looked back to Father at the end of the room. Then an outstretched palm signaled that the conversation would go no further. A cold unease wrapped around him, and he turned, making his way forcefully slow to the door.

As it closed behind him, he felt the thickness of the room tear away. He walked down the hall and found himself making his way towards his room. Somehow Father knew. He was sure of it. A few minutes later he was standing at his window peering out into the trees beyond. He had seen the grave and couldn't shake a feeling that rested in the back of his mind, whispering softly to him that the corpses and children that decided to leave were connected.

After a moment he turned and made his way to the small desk, picking up the latest book issued to him by Isabella and found his way to his bed. He opened the flaps, glancing one last time out the window before sinking into the weathered pages in his hands.

THE CEREMONY

Carlos was pulled from the pages of his book by the sound of children making their way noisily through the hallway slowly filtered into the room. He looked up, realizing it was late afternoon as his gaze moved to the window and he noticed the swirl of light grey on the horizon. He sat there for a moment before closing the story he was now over halfway through and rose to his feet. He set the book down and made his way into the hallway, entering into the flow of children as they walked noisily towards the dining hall. As he exited, closing the door to his room behind him, he could feel a strange hum in the air, an excitement that danced through the halls layered with curiosity and sadness. There was an energy of fear and admiration hanging thickly as some of the children outwardly thought the idea of leaving foolish, and others quietly coveted it. He turned right and followed the flowing mass of chattering youths. Minutes later he was taking his seat next to Isabella who had already been, as usual, one of the first to arrive.

"So, a fancy dinner?" he asked, pulling his chair in as his senses were teased provocatively by the fresh arrangements of cut fruit and warm cakes.

"I've only seen one other leave," Isabella replied, her eyes locked suspiciously to the door at the end that

Father was sure to appear from any moment. "But yeah, this is how it was."

By the time her sentence had finished the room began to buzz as a girl slightly older than her entered the room. She was frail, her slender features masked by a length of ebony hair that fell to her waist; a mane so dark it seemed to absorb the light around it. Carlos listened as one of the children at the table whispered to another loudly that the girl was Marianna. He let his gaze stay with the girl for a moment as a crowd of children rose and began to gather around her, their words and shouts all lost to a growing din of echoes throughout the room. He realized at that moment that even though there was only a few dozen children, many of them didn't have the faintest clue who any of the others were. His thought was interrupted by the sound of the back door creaking opened suddenly, the building crescendo in the room fading away as Father entered, making his way to his seat at the head of the main table. "Please," he said, extending his hands to them. "Take your seats."

There was a quick shuffling as the children made their way back and settled in, a long exaggerated groan filling the room as their chairs all slid inwards at once. Then the room fell silent, dozens of pairs of eyes all peering intently at the man standing at the front.

"It is on these days," Father began, his words rolling smoothly through the air, the low timbre of his voice reverberating off the walls surrounding them. "That sadness fills my chest the most." All eyes were locked to him. "Not because one of us is leaving, but because there will again be one less laughter that will ring through the halls, one less pair of feet playing on the grounds, one less person that we may find comfort, and friendship amongst. I find sorrow on this day because there is one less child that I will be able to nurture, and care for." He paused, his gaze moving to Mariana. "Please my child, would you stand for us?"

Mariana rose, her gaze held to Father's for a moment before breaking it to quickly glance around the room.

Father continued, his powerful words pressing into the children's chests as he spoke. "Mariana came to us three years ago. Her family was abusive, her uncle... *beyond* forgiveness. But like you all, she was led here; found her way to this island, where she found refuge amongst others just like herself; gentle souls cast out by an uncaring world." He smiled, his eyes soft as they gazed upon the child standing with her arms pressed firmly to the sides of her blue summer dress. "And while she was here amongst us, she touched many of our lives, and became a friend to many of you. As are all of you, she is special, to the rest of you, and to myself."

He looked at her for a brief pause before telling her

that she could be seated. The air in the room held the lightness of a funeral eulogy.

"But alas," he continued, "now the time has come, which unfortunately, will happen with all of you, in which she feels as though she is ready to rejoin the world that has been waiting. She no longer feels as though this island is enough, and wishes to find a new life elsewhere."

Carlos fidgeted in his seat and glanced to his right to see an uncomfortable squint flash through Isabella's eyes. He could sense that Father was hiding a razor thin strip of sarcasm behind his delivery.

"Now we cannot become upset by her decision, because it is just that; *her* decision. Mariana and I talked in great length about the hardships that she will face as she attempts to reintegrate herself into the society of man. And she is well aware of the risks. So as I have always done, and always will, I will escort her to the docks, ensuring that the beast does not relieve her of her life, and will ensure that she is returned to the world it is she wishes to rejoin." He paused, his gaze again falling to Mariana. "We will *all* miss you Mariana. You are a sister to your friends and a daughter to myself, and I truly regret your decision to leave. But I respect it, and will remember you always." He smiled, reaching out to take up his glass which he held high above the table in front of him, gesturing for the others to do the same. "To your memory, and may you find whatever it is that you are seeking." He took his sip, the rest of the children following suit. "Now," he said, a wide smile moving across his lips. "Let our cloud of sadness be dissipated, and allow us to send our sister off with gallant festivity."

Father slowly took his seat as the room erupted into a series of loud clapping and cheers, followed by the returning rumble of chatter as everyone began reaching out for the food that had sat taunting them.

Carlos paused as he set a sweet roll on the plate in front of him. The pit flashed through his memory and he couldn't help feeling that Father's words had felt a touch sinister. His hand hovered for a moment before he set them in his lap, his gaze lost in the ivory cream that the roll sat upon.

"Are you ok Carlos?" Isabella said after a moment, realizing her friend sat nearly catatonic next to her.

"Huh?" Carlos replied, turning his gaze to her.

"Are you alright? You seem a bit, off."

"Uh, yeah," he lied, shaking the cobwebs that held his thoughts in place free. "Just thinking about the orphanage…"

Isabella stared at him for a moment before reaching out to grab a pitcher of strawberry agua fresca and filling her glass. For the next hour they sat in the dining hall, listening to the rumble of voices and occasional staccato bursts of laughter that would erupt. They ate their fill and enjoyed the atmosphere, watching as others would rise and make their way to the other girl, saying their goodbyes and giving words of encouragement. Then when some of the children began leaving, heading back to their daily routine or jobs, Carlos looked at Isabella and said, "I'm gonna go for a walk before the sun goes down."

Isabella nodded, wiping her hands on the cloth napkin across her lap. "I've got a few things I need to finish up in the library," she replied. "I guess I'll see you a little later?"

Carlos nodded with a weak smile. "Yeah." He slid his chair out and made his way to the exit. It was a short time later that he again found himself standing in front of the shrub covered log, and the path that lead into the woods.

THE MONSTER

An hour had passed before the hairs on his arms rose to the smell of ancient decay—peat moss mixed with wet cloth and the coppery smell of dried blood. He realized he had returned to the corpse filled pit. As he approached his face was blank, his emotions writhing just beneath the gooseflesh that enveloped him. He didn't know why he had returned, but at the same time, he understood fully well. He needed to see if what he had seen before was real, and now, as he stood at the edge of the gaping hole filled with a macabre latticework of rotting flesh and dried bones, he knew fully well it was. But why..?

He stood there for a moment, realizing that the sun would nearly be down by the time he got back when a distant sound whispered past his ears. He froze, still as death, with his breath held in his lungs as his ears strained to locate the piercing sound that had just ripped his gaze from the hole and brought the hair on the back of his neck to attention. Statuesque he stood, an invisible pillar standing against a backdrop of giant trees. Then the sound filtered through again. This time he knew what it was.

Carlos turned and darted into a cluster of brush obscured trees that stood a short distance away. The distant sound of a girl screaming still rang in his ears as it was replaced by something bigger, something heavy and loud, a crunching, slamming cadence of approach from the direction the cry had ended in. He sat in the brush, his eyes gazing through a small section where the leaves had fallen bare, leaving a crosshatch of twigs just wide enough to see through, but tight enough to hide his frightened gaze. Then the phantom stepped out of the woods directly across the pit.

Carlos froze, his hands beginning to shake as his back tensed with wave after wave of trembling fear. Across the chasm of rot stood the monster that stalked the woods. The creature stood, standing jet black over the uncountable death, thick hair that covered its body bristling lightly in the breeze that had begun to blow past. There was a thin strip of silver running down one side of its canine like face and its eyes burned green against the colorless spaces surrounding them. It stood erect, almost human in stance, but the face was heavy and wolf-like, a blunted muzzle just below its deeply set gaze. At the end of its thick, fur covered arm, dangling limply from its clawed grip, was the corpse of the young girl that just a short time before, had stood smiling, the center of attention at a dinner held in her honor.

Carlos stared, his breath a shuddered stagger of quick inhales and equally short exhales. His arms and legs trembled and he pressed his teeth together tightly to keep the sound of chattering from escaping. He stared, his eyes wide and unblinking as the monster held the girl that had been sitting three tables away just a few hours earlier up and tore the top part of her dress away, exposing her bare chest. Then, in the same manner a person would bite a chunk from a ripe apple, it buried its muzzle into her chest. The sickening crunch of bone and rending flesh flooded across the clearing and drew tears from the corner of Carlos's paralyzed eyes. It stood there, taking another two chunks out of the small girl, flipping the broken bones of her ribcage aside with a flick of its head and then lifted its other paw to yank the tiny heart from the gaping wound. Silently it stood, staring at the dripping organ, and as carelessly as one would cast away the core of an eaten apple, tossed the body of the girl into the pit, its gaze not once averting from the glistening organ. Carlos stared as the beast gazed upon the child's heart as if studying and admiring it at the same time, watching as it slowly brought it to its snout and began taking small, delicate chunks out of it, pausing as it chewed the raw meat slowly, savoring the taste of innocence and youth.

Carlos sat horrified. The brush around him seemed to peel away as his fear threatened to expose him. He shuddered, watching as the nightmare wrapped in fur and teeth devoured the girl's essence. He stared as the girl lay at an odd angle, another corpse added to a pile of dead children.

When the creature finished devouring the last of the young girl's heart it stopped, its nose flicking up and down as the sides of its mouth curled up into a snarl. Carlos stayed motionless, his breath held captive in his lungs as the creature across the pit sniffed the air, a low growl rumbling deep within its massive frame. Its eyes locked to the bushes that Carlos was hiding in, its pupils shrinking as its gaze zeroed in on where he was crouched. It knew he was there. He was sure of it, and now he was going to be added to the pit.

Carlos slowly pulled his face back, attempting to obscure himself even deeper into the thick growth, holding his breath as he did. Then as quickly as the creature had appeared, it turned and rushed into the woods beyond, disappearing with the crushing loudness that it had arrived with.

Carlos sat in the bush for the next hour. His legs were cramped and his cheeks burned where the tears had left dried streaks of salt. By the time he gathered the courage to make his escape, the sun had already begun to fall beyond the horizon.

He pulled himself free from the bush and stood there silent for a moment before turning to the path and again, running as fast as he could towards the safety of the castle.

A short time later that he was diving into the end of the log and scrambling towards the grassy field on the other side.

A GRISLY TALE

As Carlos entered the castle he realized that he was again covered in dirt and countless scratches from where he had dove behind the tiny, thorn covered shrubs. His skin itched where the thin streaks of pink and red crisscrossed his exposed arms and face. He rubbed his arm as another child walked past, giving him a puzzled look as they did. Then he entered the library.

"Isabella," he called out, stepping towards the middle of the room.

A second later his friend appeared behind the main pillar. "Hi Carlos," she began, pausing as the marks across his face and debris still contained in his hair made her stop. "What happened now? I suppose you were cleaning the fountain again...?" A hint of sarcasm layered the tone of his friend's voice, and he could see from the look in her eyes exactly how bad he looked.

"I need to talk to you..," he replied, his voice low and flat.

She set the book down that she held in her hand and walked towards him.

"Not here," he said as she approached.

Something in his eyes brought a nervous flutter into her chest. Something was wrong, very wrong. "Carlos you're scaring me..."

He let his gaze fall to the floor for a moment before

lifting it to hers. "The fountain," he said, turning to make his way back outside, rubbing his left arm as he did.

She followed.

A short time later the pair were sitting on the lip of the marble basin. The last lingering bit of sunlight clung to the horizon in purple desperation as he looked around the yard and up to the second story ledge to make sure the tiny creature that acted as Father's spy wasn't listening in on their conversation. Overhead the stars had already come out from their nightly slumber.

"I went into the woods," he said, words low as he locked his eyes to hers.

"Carlos!" she exclaimed lowly, "You know that's not allowed. You could have been killed."

"I know," he replied, again breaking her gaze to glance around. "The monster is real," he said, leaning in closer as his words fell to a whisper. "And—"

Isabella stared at him unblinking as sadness choked his words. She felt as if a cool breeze had just touched her skin that was covered in a thin layer of sweat still clinging on from her work in the library.

"It's worse... There's bodies," he said, his gaze moving to the woods and back.

"What are you talking about Carlos? What bodies..?"

"There's hundreds. A giant pit. A hole in the ground, filled with them. Their all dead. The monster is real."

Isabella stared, a single slow blink moving her eyes against her flush face.

"That girl, Mariana. She's dead. I watched it tear her heart out and eat it." He paused, his gaze falling to the grass at the base of the fountain. "She never made it to the docks..."

"What..?" Her face paled. "What about Father?" she asked, her brow furrowing as her words whispered out.

"I didn't see him," he replied, the vision of the fur covered monster still fresh in his mind. "Maybe, maybe he ran. He told me that he had some, deal with the island. That he knew when the beast would be out. Maybe it surprised them."

"We should check his room. Let's see if he's ok," she said, her head turning to the mansion.

"We can't... It's forbidden to enter the woods, and I don't want to find out what the punishment is for it. I may be sent away, or worse..."

"Look," she said after a moment, quickly scanning the area around them again. "Are you *sure* what you saw? Could you have been... imagining things? Was it just a really bad dream? Because I've had dreams that I awoke from and though they were real; dreams that were just as real as this. I think this island has something to do with it."

"It wasn't a dream," Carlos whispered, his words steady and fierce.

"Ok... Ok."

Carlos took a deep breath, exhaling slow and deliberately. "Please... You have to trust me. I saw it."

The pair stared at each other as the last of the sunlight began to fade away, the sky above the woods beginning to blend in with the top of the canopy.

"I need to see it."

Carlos looks up, shock hitting his face. "What? No!"

"I have to. And tomorrow, you're going to show me, or I'm going to go into the woods and look for myself." Her words were strong and unwavering. If there was something like that on the island, then she had to see it with her own eyes. She needed to. She had felt from the moment that she arrived that something was *off*. If there was an explanation, then she had to know. She was tired of wondering.

"No!" he snapped quickly. "It's not safe."

"Why?" Isabella snapped. "Because you're a boy and I'm not?"

"No... It's not like that... I just don't think. I don't think we should go back there. That's all."

Instantly regret began to fill him as his hands fidgeted in his lap, his gaze moving to the trees.

"I have to see," she replied, her voice still resolute. "What if those who decide to leave, are just food for the creature in the woods, sacrifices? What if none of us really get to leave? If what Father says is not true and we are just being given to the monster in the woods? No. I have to know." She paused. "He told you about a pact with the island. What if we're part of that pact? There are too many questions without answers here." She pulled her gaze away from him, slowly settling it on the woods beyond.

Carlos felt the regret growing bigger inside him. He knew he should have just gone to his room, bathed and then gone to sleep. Telling her had done nothing but place the risk of losing her on him. If he lost her... If the first person that he considered as his friend was killed, or worse... But he knew her very well. If he didn't show her, didn't go with her, then she would make her way there herself. He had made a mistake telling her. "We go first thing in the morning." He reached out, clasping his hands on hers. "But if we hear anything, then we turn, and we run back here as fast as we can. I'll distract it and you run. I can't let anything happen to you."

Isabella nodded, her eyes again glancing to the trees beyond before locking back to his. She gently took his hands in hers, squeezing softly. The boy that now stood in front of her had changed. No longer was he the weak, hunched shouldered shape drifting alone in the halls. He had become brave, finding a solid resolution. There was something almost attractive about it that caused her to smile softly. "Nothing will happen as long as we're together."

Carlos nodded. He felt no reassurance in her words. After what he had seen, nothing on this island was an assurance.

She looked past him at the castle, scanning for the small winged creature. "Tell me what you saw Carlos. From the beginning."

Carlos explained in detail what he had seen, from the monstrous canine appearance of the creature to the careless manner in which it tossed the girl aside, eating only her heart. He told her about the blazing eyes and feeling that it had almost sensed his presence. He told her about finding the pit the first time and warned her of the smell. By the time he was finished with his tale the sunlight was gone completely gone and darkness had blanketed the yard.

Carlos looked uneasily at the trees, standing up as he did; the image of two flashing emeralds filling his memory. "We should be going," he said. "We're gonna be late for dinner and I still need to wash up."

Isabella nodded, standing to follow her friend.

As much as he wished it so, that the monster that now hunted the dark spaces of his mind, wasn't an illusion or fantastical daydream. It was very much real, and it was large, and hungry.

They finished their dinner a short time later and made their way to their rooms. Carlos drew the curtains and blocked out the world beyond, making his way to the safety of his bed. As he was falling asleep he heard what sounded like the distant howl of a wolf filtering out of the trees and pulled the covers up to cover his head.

DEVOURED DREAMS

The next morning the room buzzed around them as the pair ate silently, conversations floating past disinterested ears. Both of them ate with their heads down, looking up only occasionally to share a silent exchange that needed no words. When they had finished they stood up and made their way outside. Both of them knew what they had to do, and the fear of it worked between them in a string of twisting knots. A short time later, Carlos showed her the entrance to the woods and they crawled through, looking behind as each of them made their way in. They followed the trail, walking silently as they did until they reached the edge of the pit. As they approached a long hour later, Isabella slowed, her hand raising up to her mouth as she stepped forward.

Carlos stood back, just out of reach of the sight below as his friend stepped closer, both hands now covering her nose and mouth. He held his place as she peered down into the violent abyss filled with desecration and fear, and heard her release a small gasp.

Isabella stood there, sadness, terror and rage welling inside of her as tears slowly rolled down her soft cheeks. The brutal truth of their situation stabbed into her relentlessly. The entire time she thought that as the children became too old, they were sent away, to return to the worlds they had arrived from. She had the feeling that something was strange, but this—what lay before her—this was beyond that. Now as she stared down at the bloating corpse of the young girl, Mariana, her skin a light shade of puffed grey, and another whom had been *released* a few months prior, she was pummeled with the reality of what *truly* happened when a child decided to leave. They found themselves in this pit, their hearts torn from their chest, a tiny meal for the beast that stalked the woods around them.

Carlos walked up and placed his hand on her shoulder. She flinched, her shock-filled gaze locking to his. He slowly nodded. He knew exactly what it was that she was feeling. He had stood there days prior feeling the same things. He knew that even the most caring words would not console the staunch reality before them.

"We should go," he whispered, squeezing her shoulder slightly.

Barely allowing her head to move, she nodded.

Snap

Carlos and Isabella whipped their faces around, both pressing in to cling to one another as the sound of the stick snapping underfoot ripped their attention to the trail they had followed there. Together they stood paralyzed, Isabella's arms wrapped around him, their eyes locked in fear as the sight in front of them registered.

Standing a short distance away was a boy, older than Carlos by at least ten years. He was tall, his frame thin and he wore clothing that had obviously not been changed in a very long time. His face was gaunt, highlighted by a short layer of scruff, and his hair hung in shaggy curls around his shoulders. His eyes were a dull blue, and centered between them was a bow with its string drawn tight, an arrow resting on a single, curled finger.

The young man stared at them, studying their huddled forms, his eyes shifting between them. Then he spoke. "It's not safe here," he whispered just loudly enough for them to hear as his eyes shifted cautiously through the trees around them. "Follow."

A SURVIVOR

Arias had been hunting the woods, as he had done so for the last seven forgotten years; time that had passed silently by since he had escaped the castle. This day was no different than the others that had crept languidly by; leave his shelter, scavenge for berries and nuts, walk the woods with his bow in hopes for a squirrel or wild rabbit to feed him. When he lived amongst the others food had been plenty, all his cares lost to lazy days and childhood daydreams, but then he had become older, and began to ask the wrong questions. That had led him on his walk through the woods, Father accompanying him, and to his narrow escape, and now his refuge alone, captive to the island, and the sprawling growth.

It was today that he had been quietly completing his routine when first; a smell wafted past his nose, floral and light, sweet and inviting. Then he heard the footsteps.

Arias ducked behind a small brush and waited. Moments later a pair of children made their way past. *You're too loud!* he screamed to himself silently. *And your perfume is going to attract the beast. You're inviting him to us.*

The pair made their way past and he listened to their light conversation. They spoke in hushed tones, which was good, but if he could hear them, then...

He watched as they traveled the path that he had created while scavenging the castle in the beginning; in the time shortly after his escape. He knew what that path would lead to, and only hoped that the scream that was sure to follow didn't bring the beast down upon them. He had never seen it during the daytime, but that was what had kept him alive all these years; not taking unnecessary chances.

The pair had reached the pit, and he watched from a short ways behind, taking immediate notice that the boy was showing the young girl what he had obviously found earlier. Then he recognized him. The boy standing next to her had been the one he had seen hiding in the bushes days prior. He had almost been killed, his scent caught by the beast, when Arias had wasted an arrow shooting it deep into the woods to draw the monster away long enough for him to escape.

He stood there watching, realizing that this could be a chance for him to make allies in the castle, a means to food, or even more so, escape. The thoughts pummeled him with unbound force. He watched silently as the pair stood, gazing upon them as the boy moved in to console the trembling girl. Then he rose up and made his way towards them, the need to interact driving him closer as he drew the string on his bow back. Again, no unnecessary risks. Deliberately he reached his foot out and allowed it to rest heavily on a small pile of dried twigs.

Snap

Carlos glanced nervously at Isabella, a strange feeling growing inside him that screamed angrily at him for putting her in this situation, and at the same time, calmly whispered that he now needed to act as her protector. They had no idea who this boy was, or where he had come from. The only thing that they shared unspoken between them, was that if he had meant them harm, then his bow would have been used long before he revealed himself.

She nodded and they turned, following silently behind the boy who pushed a large fallen branch aside and led them onto a barely visible trail that led in a different direction. For the next twenty minutes they walked in silence, the boy not looking back once as they stepped quickly through the undergrowth and layer of fresh plants that attempted to bloom across the tiny foot path. Both of them took notice that it was only their steps that created the noise. The boy was nearly silent as he walked. The forest was empty, save for the distant chirps and soft crunching underfoot, and time was lost as they made their way through the trees. They were being led somewhere, and with every step Carlos felt the apprehension growing palpable. As he was about to speak up, his curiosity and fear of their destination driving into him, the youth stopped, turning to eye each of them nervously for a moment before pulling a large shrub aside and exposing a small tunnel that led beneath a massive fallen tree.

"Down here," he said, turning to make his way inward after a quick scan of the area behind them.

Carlos swallowed heavily, looking to Isabella for a breaths time before following the boy inwards.

The tunnel was small, just large enough for them to walk through upright. It smelled of moist earth and moss, and was shorter than Carlos had expected. A short distance down the tunnel opened up into an equally small room that had been dug out of the earth beneath the large tree above. Light came from a single source, a hole in the ceiling and casted down to illuminate the room. There was a pile of cloth in a back corner that Carlos could tell the boy had been using as a sleeping area, and a small, shabbily built table that contained a large collection of herbs and plants, a makeshift bow leaning against it, with a small pile of handmade arrows at its base. Standing across from it was a basket full of fresh fruits. Carlos noticed a handful of dishes and cups that he immediately recognized as being from the castle.

He stared, his eyes moving slowly around the room before settling on the young man who had set his bow down and was pulling two evenly cut tree stumps from beneath a plank of wood acting as a shelf. He motioned to them. "I don't have visitors," the boy said, his dirty face scrunching inwards as he spoke. "Please," he said, motioning towards the crude seats.

Carlos and Isabella took a seat on the stumps and glanced at each other quickly again.

"Who are you?" Isabella asked, taking notice of his familiar accent. "Is this your home?"

The boy stared blankly at her for a moment before a hint of confusion flashed past. "Home," the boy scoffed with a single shake of his head. "No," he replied, his eyes moving to meet hers. "This is where I hide."

There was a pause, a moment of silence that filled the room, pressing into their ears. As the pressure built Carlos could feel the tension becoming thicker with every beat of his heart. When he was to the point of bursting he looked up and spoke.

"How long have you been out here?" he asked, still shocked to see another person much older than anyone at the mansion.

"I don't know," the boy replied. "I stopped counting a very long time ago." He paused, his gaze moving to a small section of wall with tally marks that ran from eye level, halfway down to the floor. "I was eleven when I first arrived on this island. It feels so long ago..."

Carlos watched as Isabella stood and slowly made her way around the room, examining the small articles that were strewn about. The boy shifted nervously but didn't say anything. As Carlos continued speaking with him, her gaze fell upon a sight she was all too familiar with, her attention fading from their conversation to the leather bound object on the table; a single book lying atop a makeshift desk. Slowly she moved towards it, her hand reaching out to open the cover. Familiar words scrawled across the open pages, the Spanish words written in nearly perfect calligraphy, flowing in loops and swirls.

My name is Santiago Davilla, and this is my account. It was the year of our Lord; 1602, when the ship I was on set sail to Solent. I was a boy, no more than 12, working as a cleaner in the cabin. It was after a raging defeat that our captain sought return to Spain, escaping death at the hands of the Dutch, only to have the sea destroy the remainder of our ships off the coast of Scotland. It was here that our ship, the rest of the crew, and the spoils they had obtained, found their way to the bottom of the sea, and I found myself waking ashore this strange island.

The boy stopped as the look on Carlos's face turned from scared to puzzled, his eyes locked on his friend.

"What is this?" she asked, her gaze rising from the battered pages at the momentary sound of silence.

"His journal," the boy replied. "Father's."

"Where did you get this?"

The boy stared at her nervously for a moment, his expression slowly fading to a blank remembrance. "We stole it..."

"We? Who's we?"

Sadness washed across his face. "Martín and I."

Carlos instinctively looked back to the entrance before moving his gaze back to the boy. "What do you know of this island?"

Suddenly the boy became nervous, a silent apprehension working through him. "Take it. Take the book. It will explain everything."

Isabella stood there, her driving curiosity unquelled.

"Who is Martín? Who are you, and how did you steal this from Father?" Her words were delivered in a snap, his obfuscation beginning to irritate her.

The boy stared at her, whatever emotions flowing through him held behind a mask of blank confusion. She could see his mind racing through his past, countless faces and voices flooding in, but he sat silently, the images held to himself. "My name is Arias. I escaped." The boy paused as Isabella made her way next to Carlos, the book still held in her grasp. A look of fear flashed past his eyes as he glanced quickly at the book and then back to them. "Take it. Read it. When you know the truth, return here. We will speak." His eyes glanced nervously between them, shooting to the entrance of his room. "Now leave. It's not safe."

"Come with us," Carlos said.

He couldn't understand why the boy had moved to the woods, struggling to live with the beast, and the elements, and lack of food when the castle was less than an hour walk away.

"No!" The boy's word was sharp, cracking through the small den. As he exclaimed he shrunk back, his gaze falling to the tunnel leading up. Fear crossed through his eyes and for a moment he held his breath. "Please—go."

Isabella could see the panic building in him, a fox with its leg caught in a snare. She reached out and gently put her hand around Carlos's arm before he could form his next question. "We should go," she said, not taking her eyes off the other.

Carlos nodded. "We will return," he said, the queasy feeling of pity brushing past. "We'll bring you food, and some blankets."

"Let's go," Isabella repeated, slowly tugging on his arm.

The boy stayed quiet, his gaze moving between both of them, watching as they turned and made their way back to the surface. When the pair had left he moved to the entrance of the tunnel and looked around, his nose sniffing the air a few short puffs and then pulled the brush back in front and made his way back down.

He sat there, his eyes locked to the blank space on the desk where the book had sat. A strange feeling of loss and comfort coursed through him. His mind, however, raced with questions. But more than that, something else had stirred in him. The pair offered him something that if only for a moment was what he had long forgotten a necessity, companionship. He hoped they would return. He was tired of watching the pit grow.

"Who is that?" Carlos asked a short time later as they made their way quietly through the trees. He knew that she had no answer either but the question was burning in him.

"Whoever it is," she replied, glancing behind her. "He's been out here for quite some time. Did you see his clothing?"

"And the way he looked at us... It was like he hasn't seen another person in years."

"Whatever is in these pages, it has him scared," she said, lightly squeezing her fingers against the soft leather.

"No," Carlos replied softly, barely above a whisper. "It's what's in these woods that has him scared."

The pair made their way back to the log leading to the castle grounds. Carlos crawled through first, pausing before exiting to make sure any unwanted eyes weren't upon them. When he was satisfied it was clear, he crawled out into the grass, keeping watch while Isabella did the same. Then the pair started their way back.

They entered the castle, both of them instinctually making their way towards their rooms. They walked silently until they reach his room and then stopped.

He was about to form a question when Isabella flashed a look that cut his words short.

"I've got some reading to do," she said. "I'll see you at supper."

Carlos nodded, watching as she turned and walked away. He admired how strong she was. He like that she was pretty, and appeared dainty and light, but beneath the soft exterior lay something that had been hardened by time and experiences. She wasn't like the other girls. He felt safe with her, and as he made his way into his room and closed the door, only hoped that she felt the same.

THE JOURNAL

Isabella closed the door to her room and made her way to the desk, listening for a moment to make sure no one was approaching, before pulling the book from where it was hidden in her dress and setting it on the table. She opened the front cover and let her gaze fall to the faded script.

My name is Santiago Davilla, and this is my account. It was the year of our Lord; 1602, when the ship I had been assigned to set sail to Solent. I was a boy, no more than 12, working as a cleaner in the cabin, and servant to the Captain. It was after a raging defeat that he sought return to Spain, escaping death at the hands of the Dutch, only to have our ship, and the others that made follow, destroyed by storms off the coast of Scotland. It was here that our ship, the rest of the crew, and the spoils they had obtained, found their way to the bottom of the sea, and I found myself waking ashore this strange island. That was one hundred and sixty years ago.

It was not until now that I felt compelled to put this story to page. However, if the day shall ever come where I find myself granted the freedom of death, my only wish is to ensure that he who is to replace me, be given the warning I never received, of what this position means, and that, which it holds. This island offers not eternal life, but merely unending death.

I had made my way inwards when I first arrived. I was astonished by the beauty of the isle. The lush green, the chorus of birds in the forest, the endless supply of game. It was without question, the most beautiful island I had ever set foot upon. It was a short time later, that I happened upon the castle; that which I now inhabit; a massive casona of outstanding proportions standing in pristine condition as if waiting to be found. I can still remember the awe that filled me whence I first set my gaze upon the out of place castle sitting alone and abandoned. The palace was barren, no life having appeared to have touched in in an uncountable amount of time. I wandered the hallways for days, exploring every nook and cranny, admiring the artwork that somehow, still hung intact. It was weeks before I found my way to the fourth floor, and the room guarded by wolves. If I could return to the time of my youth, I would beg myself not to open that door; to seal it up behind a wall for all eternity. But here I sit, and that time is long past. It was in that room that I was met by a creature the likes of which I have in all my years at sea, exploring the distant lands, had yet to see. One that was almost human like in its tiny, scaled and winged form. It was here, that I met the devil that inhabits this land; the one who watches the isle.

This creature is far from the La Arjana of the old tales; kind and gentle, filled with wonder and song. No... I would come to find out that this creature, this demon, was malevolence manifest. I fear I did not find this out before agreeing to an offer no mortal man could resist, a bargain—one that I would long come to regret, spoken in a tongue I could not comprehend, spoken more to the mind than the ear, a deal that would leave me locked, bound to this island, a servant to the tiny monster. In exchange for the promise of endless life, I was needed only to inhabit the mansion and provide food for the creature, food which it itself would harvest. I was to ensure that the castle was maintained and watch over the livestock, as the creature referred. Had I known then what that source of nourishment would be, what that livestock was to be, I would have led myself back out to sea and gladly joined my crew at the bottom.

When the first child arrived I took it in as my own, surely under the thought that it was a castaway that arrived as I myself had those months ago. Then, as the next few years went by, a small handful of others arrived, all still but children. The creature began to become more and more agitated as a voice—no, a presence, began to grow in my own mind. I could hear the voice, low and angry, speaking to me just beyond the fringes of thought, urging me to kill, to end the boy's life and feast upon him, allowing his blood to seep into the earth, to feed the island. Then one day, shortly after the fifth child appeared, the creature found me in my room and *whispered again in that tongue that that pierces the mind, the one I fear only I am cursed to hear. I was to kill the children so that it may feast on their bones. That was the food I was to provide. I refused. It was at that moment that the nature of my bargain was revealed, and my hunger began. No longer would the endless food of the island nourish me. The meats and vegetables I ate only served to make me sick, my body rejecting it not past the smell. My hunger grew and grew until I thought the blind fury of it would end me, the voice in the back of my mind growing to a roar. It was the week following that I took that boy; Armando—I still remember his name, into the woods to hunt as we had for those years prior. Only on this day however, I changed. My body contorted, shifting painfully as it grew, morphing as course hair pierced its way from beneath my skin, covering me in a thick black coat. I became a beast, the monster that writhes in the darkest recesses of my mind tearing its way forward, taking control and leaving me to watch powerlessly as it stalked and killed. My self-control was lost to the blinding hunger, and I hunted the boy that I had raised and nurtured. I hunted him, knowing what I was doing, watching in horror from behind eyes that were mine, that I no longer controlled. I stared helplessly from within as the monster killed him. I took his life, and the beast I had become, devoured that boy's heart. For the first time in months, my hunger had been satiated. It was there, in the woods that day, the blood of that boy still fresh on my chin, as I watched the tiny demon feed upon the exposed bones, that I realized. Forever, this Island would be my prison.*

Isabella set the book down on the table, her hands trembling. Slowly she reached out and closed the cover. She felt dizzy, the room around her swimming as the words reverberated over and over in her mind. Father was the beast. He was the one filling the pit, and the tiny creature they referred to as his pet, could not have been more the opposite. Father, himself, was the pet.

Slowly she stood, wrapping the book in a handkerchief and made her way down the hall to Carlos's room. She reached her hand out, pausing for a moment in an attempt to compose herself before knocking.

"We need to go back. We need to speak with him."

Carlos stood just inside the doorway, staring at his friend whose face had become drawn and pale. He knew something was terribly wrong; that whatever it was that she found contained in the pages of the book were worse than the things he had already known. There was no arguing against the eyes that pierced coldly back at him, so with reluctant movement, he responded with a small nod and a whispered ok.

He stepped out and closed the door behind him. It was late, and most of the children had already made their way back to their rooms for the evening. Going through the woods now only invited trouble. He knew it was dangerous, but he was quickly realizing, everything on the island was. This at least, they were semi in control of.

"What did it say?" he asked as they entered the foyer.

She stopped, turning to him, her response a silent gaze that held uncomprehending fear behind it. Then she shook her head slowly and turned, continuing her way outside.

THE RETURN TO THE WOODS

As they made their way back through the woods she explained everything she had read, from Father's arrival, to the deal with the creature, to the killing of the children. Carlos was stunned. He felt hollow and scared, but at the same time, a sliver of pity for Father as well. He was just as much a prisoner on the island as the rest of them were. His empathy, however, did little to lighten their situation, or soften the pit filled with decay.

They made their way to where the boy's den was and slowly moved the brush aside, Isabella whispering down as Carlos stood watching around them.

"Arias?" she whispered out. "Are you there?"

Silence returned her answer.

"I think he's out," she said, glancing at Carlos who stood nervously behind her.

"You're too noisy."

Isabella snapped her head back to the tunnel to see the boy standing at the end of it, a nervous look drawn across his face. "You should not have come here. This forest is not safe at night. Ever."

She tapped Carlos and started downwards. He moved the brush back into place and followed. As they reached the bottom Isabella held the book out and asked, "How did you get this?"

Arias took a deep breath, his gaze held to the

outstretched book, shying backwards as if Isabella was attempting to hand him an ancient, cursed relic. He was not going to take the book back, and should she attempt to leave it with him, he would bury it in the deepest hole he could dig.

He swallowed hard, his gaze moving to her and then back to the book.

When she realized he wasn't going to take it she let her arms drop down and set the book in her lap as she sat on the small log where she had before.

"I knew something was wrong shortly after I arrived. I had grown suspicious of Father, and the small creature that always accompanied him. I knew from the day I arrived that something was wrong, as most of those that arrive do. But unlike the others, that feeling did not fade. One day my best friend Martín and I, came up with a plan. We would instigate a fight amongst two of the others that lived with us, which would draw the attention of the creature and Father away, using the commotion for us to sneak into his room and try to find out anything we could about him. The plan worked. The boys fought, Father and the creature made their way to the back of the mansion near the fountain, and I snuck into his room. While Martín kept watch, I searched." His gaze fell to the book in her lap. "It was in a small drawer near his bed that I found that." His gaze rose back to meet theirs. "We took it to my room and read it." He paused, the feelings he had felt that day flooding back into him, the face of his friend as they realized their true situation flashing past his eyes. "It was then that we realized we needed to escape. It was our time to leave." He paused, his brow furrowing tightly as he continued. "We didn't realize, we didn't know. No one leaves this island. No one." Again he paused. "We went to Father, and we told him that we wished to leave. He told us that he was sad to see us go, but would prepare our travels to America. There was a celebration, we danced and sang… We said our goodbyes. He led Martín and I into the woods that evening; told us that it was the only way for us to be safe traveling through. He had already spread the story of the beast roaming the woods long before." The boy stopped, glancing to the door as his ear visibly twitched, searching for a sound too faint for Carlos or Isabella to hear. Then after a moment, he began again. "Father told us that he was leading us to the docks, that a boat would be waiting to take us to America," he continued, his gaze drifting to the side as memories from his escape resurfaced, the smiling, and very dead face of his friend inches from his own grasping hold. "But we knew different, we knew the truth, and in our youthful naivety, we thought ourselves prepared. We had both concealed knives taken from the kitchen. We were simply going to wait until Father took the form of the beast, and then kill him. But it wasn't until we were already deep within the forest that we realized that Father was no longer with us." He inhaled deeply, his exhale billowing the air in the room. "That was when we heard the howl. It was big, and deep; a sound that I have come to know well these past years. We turned and ran, towards the only place we knew safe... the castle. It was a matter of minutes before Father found us, but not the Father that had led us into the woods, the one from his book. We tried to run, but Father—the beast, was faster than we could have imagined. It was moments until he caught us. We were cornered, trapped. I remember pulling my knife as he approached and slashing out. I cut him from its jaw to its chest as it leapt atop me. I knew he was going to kill me, but Martín threw a rock at his head. It was just enough to take the beast's attention off of me." He paused, the hint of a tear pondering whether or not to form in his eye. "That beast... *Father*..." He inhaled sharply again, his exhale short and heavy. "Martín sacrificed himself so that I could escape."

Carlos exchanged a long glance with Isabella, her hand slowly moving out to take his.

"I ran as fast as I could. And then I fell into the pit. I struggled to get out, trying to scramble over the countless bodies. Then I heard him approaching. I did the only thing I could think... I pulled two bodies over mine and I laid there, covered in old, rotting death as that *monster* tore the heart from Martín's chest and ate it. He threw my best friend into the pit like a used cloth. And until the sun went down, I lay there, staring into my friend's eyes…" The tear held its place as he lifted his head to look at the both of them. "Shortly after that, I found this unused den. This became my home. As you can see by the few things I have collected over time; that on occasion, I have returned to the castle. A plate left on the grounds here, a cup near the fence. But I can never return. Not now. Now that I know what he truly is."

Carlos stared blankly.

"I have heard, and witnessed countless others being killed since then. It is the same every time. A child wishes to leave, there is a celebration, and Father leads them into the woods under the promise of sending them to some faraway location. No one knows. No one ever finds out. No one ever returns."

"What are we supposed to do then?" Isabella asked, irritation slowly pressing into her words. "We can't escape. We can't tell anyone, because Father will just kill us and come up with a story of how we left and didn't say goodbye. And there is no getting off this island, because the person that would lead us from here, is the same that would keep us from leaving."

"And therein lay the problem. However, there may be a way," the boy said, staring deeply into her eyes as he spoke. "There was one who came to the island a year or so before my escape. I forget the finer details, but I remember that the boy became extremely angry one day and attacked Father in the dining hall, during the middle of dinner. There was chaos, but the boy managed to bring a knife across his face, opening his cheek from ear to chin. I can remember Father screaming, and the blood…. Some of the others tackled the boy and he was drug away. Four days later Father reappeared at dinner without so much as a scratch on his face. It was never spoken of. But when I cut him that day, while he was the beast, the wound stayed. I have seen it every time I watch him stalk these woods. So maybe, if what I believe to be is correct, then there *is* a possibility, that he can be killed, it just needs to be in the woods, and while he is the beast."

"This can't be real…" Carlos whispered, the ridiculousness of it all wearing on him.

"But it is," Arias answered quickly, a strange lucidity now bright in his eyes. "Tell me, have the seasons changed since you arrived? Is there ever a shortage on food? If we're not allowed to go into the woods, where does the meat come from? How is it, that no one has ever found this island, other than what seemingly appears to be only children? This *is* real. This place is as real as you or I, or her. And Father, is a monster that must be destroyed. If he isn't, no one will ever escape this island, and for the rest of time, more will continue to die. He needs to be destroyed."

Carlos stared at Arias. The boy who had been bordered on paranoid and feral just minutes before now stared at him lucid and sharp; a gaze that spoke his true age. He knew the boy was right, had felt it since the moment he arrived, but hearing it, hearing the words out loud, carried on another voice…

"If we attack him while he is in the mansion, then he cannot be killed. But out here—in these woods he has shown his vulnerability. Out here, he *can* be. I'm sure of it."

"We?" Isabella asked, realizing instantly that the other had drawn then into his plan.

"There is only one way to get free of this place," he replied, looking deeply into her eyes as he realized the feeling he had been having; not so much a desire for companionship as much as a hope for release. "I'm not capable of doing it alone, or I would have many years ago. The only thing I can do here, is hide, and survive. But you, the *both* of you. You can lure him out, bring him out here and keep him busy just long enough for me to kill him. That's all I need; a distraction."

Isabella found herself appalled by the sacrifice the other was suggesting from them. "Not only is it an impossible task to lure him here, but we would most assuredly be killed doing so."

"It is the only way," he replied, his eyes fixed and

unblinking. "Until he is killed, until that *monster* is killed, this island will be a prison to us all, and every child that is brought here will die."

"How?" Carlos asked, his gaze locked to the other. "How do we lead him here, and how will you kill him?

Arias moved to the desk and picked up the bow, holding it in his hands as he drew the string back. "With this."

Again silence fell over the small room. Carlos found his mind a cloud of swirling thoughts, a jumble of half-finished sentences and images that flashed with green eyes and fangs. His friend however sat silent, slowly filling with dread as the older boy's words rang true.

"One of us has to tell him we are ready to leave..."

Carlos moved his face to meet Isabella's. He couldn't believe that she had suggested the idea, or that she was even considering the other's insane plan, but his silence only confirmed what he already knew. Arias was right.

"We tell him we are ready to leave, and Arias will be waiting." She turned her gaze to the other. "We know where he feeds. We knew where the bodies are thrown. All we need to do is wait for Father to disappear and we signal you. You kill him with your bow and we're free."

The boy stared at her for a moment as her words registered. "You know it will not be that simple."

"It's the only way to lure him into these woods, and if what you say is true, the only way to get him to become the monster."

"That is one thing he *always* is," the other boy replied coldly. "It is just the beast that we need to bring out.

"I'll do it," Carlos said, his words quick and frantic. "I'll tell him I want to leave."

"Carlos..."

"It has to be me," he said, turning his gaze to his friend as his hand moved back to hers. "I can't take the risk that he kills you and we are left with nothing. You're my only friend and I can't lose you."

Isabella's face softened.

"I will be ready," the other boy said, his eyes moving between them. "Now. It is late, and it is not safe in these woods at night. We should go."

"We?"

"I will make sure you get back safely. I have lived alone out here for an uncountable amount of time. These woods are just as home to me as they are to the beast."

Carlos stood, Isabella rising a moment later.

"By the way," the boy asked as they were making their way up the tunnel. "What are your names?"

The pair turned back to look at him, pausing for a moment.

"Isabella. And this is Carlos."

The boy nodded, watching as the two turned and

made their way out.

As they walked quickly towards the mansion none of them spoke. Their minds raced with the knowledge that they had just uncovered. Isabella tried desperately to remember the faces of the children she had seen leave, those she had thought had gone either home or to some fantastical, distant place. They walked in silence until they reached the log and then stopped, Carlos and Isabella turning to Arias.

"When you are ready, find me," he said, glancing past them at the castle standing behind them. The pair nodded, turning to make their way into the log, pausing only for a moment to make sure that the creature that watched the island wasn't flitting about before crawling out and making their way towards the mansion. Overhead the moon shined downwards.

"We should talk after breakfast," Isabella said as they were making their way towards the front steps. "Meet me at the fountain right after."

"Ok," Carlos said, his reply a hoarse croak.

He watched as Isabella quickened her pace and made her way rapidly in the direction of her room. He could sense that she had been holding her emotions in and could only assume that her pillow would be wet as she drifted to sleep that night. He still struggled to compose the words he had heard. He knew he had felt something when Father had approached him that night, and when the tiny creature had been watching.

He made his way to his room and closed the door behind him, walking to the window and glancing out to the woods just long enough to close the curtains before undressing and climbing into his bed. It was hours before he finally drifted off.

In the distant woods a lone owl hooted, and a dark shape flashed unseen through the trees.

THE PLAN

Carlos lay awake staring at the dark wood of the ceiling. He had been awake for some time, a nervous excitement interlaced with apprehension and binding fear having woke him more than an hour prior. He waited until the sound of sleep laden voices and soft footsteps wafted down the hall before he slowly stood and made his way to the door. He paused, his hand clasped on the cool brass handle and took a deep breath before twisting. He made his way to the dining hall with a his steps, deliberate and slow, the soft conversations around him a muffled blur as Arias' words played in an endless loop. *No one escapes the island.* He could feel his heart beating heavily in his chest as he shuffled down the hall alongside the other children; cattle led to feed. His anxiety continued to build.

He entered the dining hall and saw Isabella sitting at the table, her light meal already nearly finished. As he sat down she glanced at him and nodded. For the first time since his arrival their meal was spent nearly in silence.

He sat eating delicately as he watched the others. They were all completely oblivious to the true nature that surrounded them, and for a moment he almost envied their ignorance. Isabella sat next to him thinking very different thoughts. Anger coursed through her, a cold spite filling her, and more than once before Carlos had arrived she had to set down her fork and remind herself that it would do nothing to help them if she stood up and screamed at the top of her lungs that they were all going to die, that Father was harvesting them for the beast, and that none of them was ever going to escape. Now the energy crackled between them, a violent static subdued in the air.

She waited for him to finish and then stood, taking her plates to the dish bins. Carlos watched her turn and made her way past him without making eye contact. He quickly followed suit, paranoid now that the slightest misstep could get them caught and their plan exposed. He made his way around the castle and saw his friend sitting atop the edge of the fountain. As he approached she glanced nervously behind her to the structure looming overhead.

"We shouldn't talk here," she said as he was about to sit.

Carlos nodded, immediately turning his gaze to the sprawling green behind him.

"I have an idea," she said, hopping off the fountain and walking past him. "Let me show you this book I've been reading."

Carlos followed Isabella to the center of the grounds where she sat down and folded the book open, glancing around them one more time.

"No one will think anything of me sharing a book with someone," she said, a smile on her face that instantly began to warm the encroaching chill inside Carlos's chest. "Even Father's pet." Her attention fell to the book as she spoke. "I've been thinking about the plan, and you're right. The only way for this to work, is to lure Father into the woods," she began, speaking as if she had already formulated the entire plan on her own. "And the only way to do that, is to either wait for another child to leave, or for one of us to tell him we wish to. If we wait for another to leave, we may not have the time to prepare, or let Arias know. The only way to be in control, is for you or me to be the child that is leaving."

Carlos began to feel a cold knot building in his stomach.

"So tomorrow, we will wait until Father's pet is close to us, and you will tell me, loud enough for it to hear, that you don't want to be here anymore, and that you want to go home. If we are right, then his pet will tell him and that will begin our plan. From there, you need but tell Father it is your wish to leave. Then, we go into the woods the next day and tell Arias."

"What if it doesn't work?" Carlos asked, his eyes pleading with her for assurance. "What if he finds out our plan somehow? Isabella..."

"He won't," Isabella said, reassurance lacing her

words. Countless children have left the isle. You will be far from the first, and he has nothing to be suspicious of. You'll be fine, Carlos." Her hand reached out and pressed on his shoulder. She found herself almost believing her own words. But in truth, she was just as scared as he was, just as unsure.

Carlos nodded.

"Carlos," she said, her hand still holding firm. "You're not the only one afraid. But we both know. No matter what. If we don't do this, all of us are going to die here. There is no question to that. This is our chance to change that. We must get everyone off of this island."

"But what if we just tell everyone, and we all attack at once?"

"First," she responded quickly, leaning forward as she spoke. "That would mean convincing everyone that what we have seen is true. Do you truly think that any of the children are going to wish to hear this? And even if we did manage to get some of them to join our cause, by the time we finished telling everyone, do you think word will not have gotten back to Father?" She shook her head, pulling her hand away. "If he finds out that we know..." She took a deep breath and closed her book. "And remember what Arias said; Father cannot be killed here in the castle. It must be when he is in his true form, and in the woods. We would simply cause a stir that would lead to our disappearing, and a quick story created about how we ran away, or left without saying goodbye. Nothing would change, and this island, and Father, would live on. I saw this back in Spain. Revolutions rarely work, and those that lead them, almost always die. No... We have to try our way."

She was right. Father had said that the island had been here long before him, and that it would be here long after he was gone. But if they could kill him, then at least the children that were there could be freed.

"We must prepare," Isabella said, glancing to the house as she spoke. "Tomorrow you will tell Father that you wish to go home. I will go to Arias while you speak with Father and the following night, we must be prepared."

Isabella folded her book into her arms and stood, turning to make her way back to the mansion.

For the next two hours Carlos sat in the grass, plucking individual blades and wondering how it was that he had come to be on the island. He had thought the orphanage had been bad, but at least there, after another few years of torment, he would be freed, alive. That was never going to happen here. But now another thought hung heavy over him. Even if they got off, none of them knew where they were, or even if the rest of the world *could* be reached. They didn't know how far they were away from anywhere else, or how much food they would need for the journey. They knew nothing. They were almost safer staying on the island then attempting to leave. But he also knew that just as much as it was chancing death by leaving, staying merely assured it.

A short time later he stood and made his way back to the castle. As he approached he saw Isabella sitting on the front steps reading. He approached and she looked up, shifting her eyes to the gargoyle that stood guard nearby. Atop its head sat the tiny winged creature. It was looking out into the yard, its ears and wings slowly twitching in the wind. Carlos glanced at the watcher above and walked towards her.

Above, the tiny creature sat as it had for ages, keeping watch over the young humans as they frolicked and danced, wasting away in an endless routine of insatiable play. The tiny humans fascinated it, yet it found them profoundly repulsive. Their flesh caused its scales to crawl, and every time it fed, there was the moment of apprehensive disgust as it peeled the skin and tissue back to reach the true delicacy; the soft marrow in their bones.

"What do you mean you want to leave!?" Isabella exclaimed, her voice just loud enough to travel to the creatures ears. "How could you leave here, it's perfect. There's endless food, no homework, no bed time... How?"

The creature snapped its attention to the pair, its gaze shifting slowly as to not bring focus to its awareness. It had heard this conversation before, and knew what it meant; another child leaving; another meal. A thin smile crept invisibly across its tiny lips as a familiar taste began to fill its mouth and its tongue ran across the back of needle sharp teeth.

Carlos stared at her for a moment before her lips pursed and she gave him a look that gestured their plan was now in motion.

"I just miss my home..." he stammered, attempting to play along with a game he had never tried. I... I just don't want to be here anymore."

"So you're just going to walk away from our friendship?"

"It's not like that," he replied, very real emotion coming to surface with her words. Instantly the feeling of a charade dissipated. "I like you a lot, and this place, I really do. I just... I can't anymore."

"And you're going to tell Father tomorrow?"

Carlos nodded. "Yes," he said, his reply struggling to form. "Tomorrow."

Isabella stood up and shook her head with a sad look on her face. "You're so selfish," she said, turning with a flip of her hair and making her way quickly inside behind a stifled sob.

Carlos stood there shocked. He wasn't ready or expecting the conversation to come so quickly, and in the way that it did. It felt real at that instant, like he truly was leaving his friend. Movement caught the corner of his eye and he watched as the creature took flight and made its way toward the castle. For a moment he felt as if the words she had spoken were true, but forced himself to realize that if she had come across as anything less, that the creature might have sensed it and their plan could be put in jeopardy. He stood motionless for a moment before walking in and making his way to his room.

For the next few hours he sat alone, staring out the window at the tufts of white drifting high above the pointed green canopy. When it was time for dinner he slowly made his way to the dining hall. He sat next to Isabella who still wore a look of sadness and anger, and was about to speak when she placed her hand on his leg under the table and squeezed once. Instantly the weight dropped from his chest and he realized that she was just very good at pretending.

Father entered the room and took a seat at his table, not giving his usual speech, but simply saying, "Let's eat". He moves his gaze to Carlos and holds it, Carlos dropping his eyes to the table in response. He could feel Father's gaze piercing into him as he sat there and knew that Father had already been informed. The creature had told him, and he was now just waiting for him to approach.

That night Carlos lay in bed for hours, pondering the

endless scenarios of the conversation; how he would start it, the questions that Father would ask, how he could keep up the facade. He had no idea how long it was before sleep finally pulled him away, and when he awoke the next morning the feeling of dread sat waiting cold in the room.

REGRET

Then next morning Carlos sat quietly at breakfast. Isabella had finished and made her way to the library. She made mention of a few books that she couldn't bear to lose if anything happened; some rare copies she was sure only existed on the isle. Carlos finished up slowly and stood to take his plate to the bins. As he turned to make his way out the boy that had first met him on the island stood there.

"Good morning," Carlos said, studying the almost blank face of the other.

"Father wishes to speak with you."

Carlos nodded as the boy turned, disappearing into the hallway. The time had arrived; he could sense it. As he slowly walked the hallway he allowed his eyes to again grace every surface. He admired the twinkle of colored light cast by the stained glass windows and the amount of detail that went into the woodwork, from the arched ceiling to the engraved baseboards. So much went into the construction of the palace, but he also knew the true darkness that all the beauty hid. Mechanically his legs brought him up the steps to the second floor. When he stopped he was standing in front of Father's door. His gaze rose, slowly locking to the thick wood that separated him from the monster behind. He stood there, listening to his own breath come out in rhythmic pulses, backed by his slowly increasing heartbeat. Fear had begun to spread its sinewy tendrils through him and he could feel the onset of panic as his reflexes told him to turn and run, to forget the entire thing and to just live out the rest of his days on the island with Isabella. But he also knew, that now, now that he knew the truth, now that he knew Father's secret, his time there would never be the same. So with that, he reached up, his hand hovering for a moment, and knocked.

Father had been seated in his chair for some time, his mind a rage of thoughts; faces that had passed, children screaming as they fled in terror. From the moment the tiny demon clicked its tongue, he had begun to steel himself for another hunt. He could feel the beast inside him becoming restless in anticipation, the low growl of excitement rumbling deep in his mind. He found himself surprised at one thing. The boy whom he had been informed about, was the most recent arrival. He was sheepish and scared, and from what he had been told, was in a much worse place before he had arrived on the island. There was something about that that made him nervous; suspicious almost. No child left this soon. So now, as he sat in his room, waiting for the boy to arrive, he worked his mind around every encounter with the child, searching for what that feeling could be when a small knock reverberated across his walls.

"Enter."

Carlos felt a shiver run past his body and he reached out to clasp his hand on the cool brass. Then he turned and slowly pushed.

"Please," Father began. "Come forward."

Carlos walked towards the end of the room, his legs liquefying with each step. He could feel the moisture dehydrating from his mouth and feared that Father would hear how loudly his heart was beating. He wondered if he knew. Would Father turn into the beast in front of him and tear his beating heart from his chest? Would he simply disappear, never to be seen again, and what would happen to Isabella?

"I understand that you are no longer happy here," Father said, a milder form of stating the truth nearly impossible. "There has been a whispering that you are thinking about leaving our home."

Carlos stared at him, tracing the lines of his face and every hair on his moustache with delicate care.

"And after such a short time, there must have been *something* to coerce this thought from you, this desire."

Carlos flinched inwardly as Father paused, his gaze piercing into him as a cat would eye a mouse with its leg snapped in a trap. Father had gotten right to the point.

"I can't help but find myself wondering what that

could have been..?"

Carlos's mind raced. He had never been a good liar, and with less than a day to think, his mind was swarming with a jumble of incohesive sentences. "I just want to go home," he whispered, the only logical thing that he could say that couldn't be followed with a snared question.

"Are you truly *that* unhappy here?" Father asked, his eyes moving to a squint for a moment. "Are the other children bothering you?"

"No," Carlos replied, his voice thin and afraid. "I just want to go."

"I hope you can understand why this sits, strange with me," he replied, still unmoving in his chair. "When you came to us, you were maltreated and abused; living in an orphanage where nothing but harm had befallen you. And now, as you are surrounded by paradise, after such a *brief* stay, you wish to leave. I find this rather difficult to comprehend."

"Embry was bad," Carlos stammered, hoping desperately that his words wouldn't trip him up and give away his plan. "But this, island, this isn't real life. It isn't how things really are. I... I just want to start living; to move on from everything and start over."

"You know that you never have to leave here," Father lied. "You know you can grow old here, beside me. This island, this home, it *is* real."

Something was still off; Father could sense it, almost smell it hanging in the air between them like the fear drenched sweat coming off the frightened youth.

Carlos struggled to keep his composure, Arias's filth covered face flashing in front of him. He knew all too well what growing old on the island meant. He knew also that the moment he began to question things, or became too clever, that Father would ensure that he didn't disrupt the nature of things. He had no question about what Father's true intentions were; the beast feeding on the hearts of children burned into his memory. Carlos had stared into the pit, gazed into the eyes of death, and peered into the empty souls of those who had fallen like flies to his web. "I just, need to go." Carlos felt a ping of relief as truth filled his words. As he stared into Father's eyes, he knew that these words had conveyed all the truth needed.

Father took a deep breath and slouched back in his chair, his gaze rising to the windows above. "It pains me greatly when one of my children wishes to leave, and two so suddenly..."

His eyes fell back to Carlos. "But" he continued. "If you wish to leave, then so be it. I will arrange for travel to wherever it is you wish to begin your new life. Back to the America's I assume?"

Carlos nodded, quickly remembering the names he had learned while at the orphanage. "New York."

"Ah. New York." Father smiled as if reminiscing about a long-lost memory, his gaze moving slowly to meet his. "No child may leave this island."

Carlos tensed.

"—not without a proper sending. Tomorrow we will celebrate your time here, as a family. Then I will escort you through the woods and see you off to your new life."

Carlos nodded once. "Thank you."

Father replied in kind, a single slow nod signifying his acceptance. He hoped desperately that the youth would change his mind. He knew what the outcome was to be, and as much as his growing hunger drove him to the point of insanity, the pain of watching another child hunted and devoured still begged for the boy to stay. Still, there was something that didn't sit well with him, something odd.

"Now. I'm sure you are anxious to tell your friends of your decision, so I won't keep you. But, if you decide to change your mind, you may do so. I will be nothing but pleased, delighted in fact."

Carlos slowly stepped backwards, anxiety resurfacing as he turned to make his way to the door.

"And Carlos," Father said, stopping him in his tracks. "Prepare yourself."

Carlos stared at the floor, Father's words digging like daggers into his back.

"The world beyond these walls is waiting for you,

and it is dark, and hungry."

Carlos felt a shiver run through him as the cold air in the room pressed against his skin. He picked up his feet one by one and walked to the door. As he opened it he glanced back to see Father sitting solitary, unmoving on his throne, eyes locked to him.

Father tried desperately, struggling to paint a picture of a world filled with malevolence and evil beyond the island. Though he had never traveled, or so much as stepped foot from this place since he arrived, it was the only way he knew of keeping the monster at bay. The longer the children stayed, the more infrequent the involuntary hunts would be. He had come to learn that the tiny creature would only gather new harvests as old ones found their way to the pit, so the longer he could keep them there, the longer it would be before the beast clawed his way out. These past days however, had proven to be a relentless feast.

Carlos entered the hallway and stopped. His legs were weak and he felt as if his heart was going to burst in his chest. He wanted to run, flee to the woods and find the boat Father spoke of, but he knew. Deep in his heart he knew. There would be no escape, only death at the hands of the beast. Slowly he turned and made his way towards the library. He needed to tell Isabella that their plan had begun. He needed to feel the comforting warmth of friendship. He walked the halls slowly, his eyes no longer grazing, but locked still to the floor as it passed beneath him. There was no comfort anymore. The moment he had expressed his desire to leave, that blanket was pulled from him, leaving him vulnerable and exposed. He shrunk with every step, the island whispering his demise through the trees and above the grass, the thin clouds overhead staring down at him through the mansion walls that closed in as he passed through them. By the time smell of parchment and leather began to fill his nose he was bordering panic.

As he entered Isabella was setting a book on the table and walking towards him. He stared at her for a moment, sadness beginning to work its way through him.

"Did you tell him?" she whispered as she approached, her gaze moving across the shelves, searching for unseen eyes.

Carlos nodded.

"Then we must tell Arias at once. Your celebration is tomorrow, we must prepare."

Carlos swallowed hard.

"It'll be fine," she said, placing her hands on his shoulders which pulled him from the haze that enshrouded him when she realized in his closeness he couldn't have been more distant. "Go tell Arias, I will tell Father there is something I wish to speak to him about regarding the library." She paused, leaning forward to look deeply into his light brown eyes. "Carlos, you are the bravest boy I have ever met, and not Father, or this island, or anything can take that away from you." She smiled, soft and genuine. "Now go, and hurry, we don't have much time."

Carlos took a deep breath and exhaled loudly, turning to make his way to the grounds and around the castle. He knew she would wait a moment before going to Father, but he wasn't sure how long she could hold conversation and he feared that after his prior conversation, Father would be keeping a closer eye on him.

He cleared the corner of the building and stopped at the fountain, his eyes carefully scanning the building and surrounding for Father's pet. When he was satisfied that he wasn't being followed he darted to the bush and scampered into the log.

Isabella counted to herself, waiting long enough for Carlos to reach the grounds before making her way to Father's room. As she reached the door she pondered; why was it that he spent most of his time in that empty room, surrounded by ancient antiques and void of all furnishings save for the chair he sat in? This struck her odd, and had since her arrival. She knew he had a bedroom, as Arias had told them, but yet, it seemed that he was almost always in the large hall. She let the question linger for a moment and then brought her hand up and knocked.

"Enter."

She made her way inwards, ignoring his greeting as she approached. She was about to start the conversation when Father spoke up.

"I understand that your friend wishes to leave us."

The comment caught her off guard, and her pace slowed.

"Is he truly not happy here?"

Father studied the girl. She was close to Carlos, and if anyone knew the true reason the boy wished to leave, it would be her. He watched her face, staring into her eyes as she searched for an answer. He could see that he had caught her off guard.

"I—Carlos is a strange boy," she replied, taking the path of truth. I've known him since he arrived, and yes, I have gotten to become quite close to him, but there's a part of him that he holds distant; a part I think will never be revealed. It's almost as if he is constantly pretending to be at peace, but inside, everything is bottled up. He has had a hard life." She paused, moments that he had described to her coming back vividly. "We all have. But he more than most."

"He has gone into the woods, hasn't he?"

Isabella froze. A ripple worked its way past every hair on her arms, slowly crawling across her shoulders to meet in the middle of her back. Fear enveloped her as she struggled to maintain her composure, fighting desperately not to betray her knowledge of the fact. "I, don't believe so," she said, her response bordering a question. She waited. She watched every line on Father's face, waiting for it to shift and the beast beneath to reveal itself; to tear into her with claws like daggers and fangs dripping with venom.

"I ask for his own safety," he replied after a moment, the sincerity in his words striking her with an odd veracity. "He was seen exiting the woods onto the grounds a few days ago. It's not safe out there, and I fear that his sense of adventure is what may have spurred his desire to leave us. There are many horrors concealed in those trees—"

The faces staring blankly up from the pit flashed through her mind, the smell rising up to twist her stomach.

"—things that could change one forever. I fear for your friend, Isabella. I fear that the path he is taking, will not end well for him."

She stood silent, staring deep into his cold grey eyes.

"Now what was it that you wished to speak to me about?"

Fear had wrapped its icy fingers around her.

Isabella slowly regained her composure, making up her story about finding more books for the library and possibly expanding to build a classroom. Outside Carlos crossed quickly through the woods.

A short time later he was standing in front of Arias's den, breathing heavily and covered in a building layer of sweat.

"Arias?" he called out, the sound of his voice startling himself, causing him to glance around quickly. "Arias, are you in there?"

A moment later the boy replied from below. "Yes."

Carlos made his way down into the den and found the youth organizing a small pile of picked nuts. As he approached the boy turned and peered cautiously at him, his gaze moving to the tunnel behind as if expecting the beast to follow.

"Where is your friend?" he asked, his eyes still locked to the tunnel.

"She's at the castle distracting Father so that I could come here." He paused, waiting for the other boys gaze to move back to him. "I came to tell you. I told Father I wished to leave. My sending will be tomorrow."

Arias stared at him for a moment before slowly letting his gaze fall to the floor. "You will be in danger," he said without blinking, his mind locked to the countless faces pressed together in the pit.

Carlos watched the boy, a pressing unease growing in him. As he stared he began to question his decision to follow the older one's advice.

Arias lifted his gaze, his features tightening as his

mind worked over the plan he had designed a thousand times. "Father will lead you into the woods at sunset," he began, his eyes locking to Carlos's. "He will lead you close to the pit. And that's where he will kill you." Arias paused, watching as fear flashed through Carlos's eyes. "That is where he will *attempt* to kill you."

The fear in Carlos's chest grew like a fire fanned by the boys words.

"He always leads them close to the pit. That way once they are dead, he does not have to travel far to dispose of their corpses. It is rare that he hunts them."

"Hunts them?" Carlos asked, the image of the beast stalking children through the woods chilling his blood and wrapping his flesh in small bristles.

"Yes," Arias replied, his voice lowering as if the woods beyond his home listened through the entrance. "There are times, though they come rare, that the beast takes control. The beast hunts like an animal. It stalks its prey through the woods, chasing them until they cannot run any further. Then it kills them, and drags their body back to the pit. But, though it is infrequent, we should prepare for it as it is a possibility."

"What do I do?" Carlos asked reluctantly, knowing that whatever the answer would be, would not be words he wanted to hear.

"You need to be prepared," Arias replied, turning to make his way to the small table. He reached out and turned back to Carlos, a large knife in his hand. "I took this from the kitchen when I left." He paused, turning the blade over in his hand for a moment as he stared blankly at the glinting silver. "Father—the beast, knows this blade well." He stepped to Carlos and handed him the knife. "Make sure you have this when Father leads you here. I will be waiting, but if I should fail, you will need it if you hope to survive.

Carlos reached out, his hand shaking as he felt the weight of the knife settle into his palm.

"Now you should go. I need to prepare."

"But I still don't know what I'm supposed to do," Carlos replied, realizing that he was no better off now than when he arrived.

"There is nothing you can do," Arias replied quietly. "Father will lead you into the woods, and he will try to kill you. We just need to keep him from doing so. And if I fail..." His gaze fell to the blade in Carlos's hand. "Then you use that, because once he brings you here, it is that, or—. Once you leave the castle, you cannot return."

"And what will you do?"

"I will be waiting," Arias replied, his gaze lowering as Carlos quickly eyed the bow behind him. "As I have been for—" The boy's words trailed off as he realized that he had no idea how long he had been hiding in the woods, waiting for the exact situation that had now been presented to him to occur.

Carlos stared at him for a moment, still feeling as confused and frightened as he did when he first entered. He had hoped that the boy would have some form of plan, that somehow his words would have given him some small amount of comfort to relieve the anxiety that was crushing him. But now as he turned and made his way back to the trail he found himself feeling even more insecure and alone. He walked through the woods, the twinkling light through the trees and shifting greens overhead as distant as the orphanage he had escaped from. His thoughts were locked solely to survival. How was he supposed to fight a massive beast with a knife? What if the boy was wrong and Father killed him just inside the woods? What would happen to Isabella, would she simply be doomed to share the same fate? The rest of his walk was slow and silent, the woods around him mocking as he tried again and again to formulate a plan, the trees whispering overhead his demise, the soft rustle of their leaves flashing with images of a death filled pit. Overhead, sitting obscured and unseen behind a dark lattice of leaf matted branches, sat Father's pet, silently watching as he made his way down the path towards the castle.

By the time Carlos made it back to the grounds it was already midday. He made his way towards the library, taking notice of a few children that stopped talking as he passed to watch him slowly walk by. One girl smiled softly at him and he could see that news of his departure was spreading like influenza. He marched through the hallway, his somber procession ending at the library doors. As he entered the library he felt the vast emptiness. The warmth that Isabella brought to the room was vacant. He knew almost instantly that she was not there by the piercing silence. Slowly he turned and started down the hall.

"Carlos!"

He turned to see Isabella walking towards him from the other end. She wore worry on her face and quickened her pace to meet him.

"We have a problem," she said, taking him by the arm and turning to make her way towards the foyer.

"What happened?" he asked, the feeling inside him that had been whispering that things couldn't get any worse now drowned out by the reality that things had.

"Father's moved the sending to this afternoon..."

"What?" Carlos asked, stopping in place.

Isabella glanced around quickly and then leaned in.

"You said that— he told me that it would be tomorrow!"

"I know!" she exclaimed in a harsh whisper. "I spoke with Father. I told him there were some things I'd like to change in the library. It was the only way I knew to keep him busy. But he started talking about you. Carlos, he knows you have gone into the woods."

"What?" Carlos said, moving forward as she grabbed his arm and drug her towards her room.

"When we finished talking he asked me if I was your friend," she continued when they were safely inside. "He told me that he feared for your safety, and that I should convince you to stay. I told him that you had already made up your mind, and that nothing I could say would change it. I talked about the library for a bit, and as I was leaving he stopped me."

"Allow me to ask you a question," Father said, his words landing across her back as she was just halfway across the room. "Carlos has never quite acclimated himself to our family, has he?"

Isabella stopped, slowly turning to face him. "No," she said, knowing anything else would have been a blatant lie, and could compromise her prior words. "I'm not sure he knows how."

"That's what I thought. So naturally, when one of you leaves, I give them a day to say their goodbye's, and spend the last amount of time enjoying the company of those they leave behind. But it seems as though, with him, that would be an unnecessary process."

Isabella stared at him, her pupils dilating as the words he had yet to speak held her breath at bay.

"I will give you the rest of the afternoon to enjoy with your friend. Tell him to prepare. Tonight we will hold his sending, and afterwards, I will escort him through the woods. New York I believe is where he said he wished to go?"

* * *

Isabella moved her hand out to Carlos's shoulder. "Father is taking you to the woods tonight."

Carlos stood shocked, his mouth slightly opening as the moisture within instantly disappeared. Arias was expecting him the next afternoon. He felt anxiety coursing through him, beating against his knees as it threatened to yank him down. "We—we have to tell Arias," he stammered, fear barely allowing the short words to be formed.

"Carlos, there's no time." Isabella took him by the forearm, grasping lightly as she turned to pull him down the hall and towards the waiting daylight spreading across the grounds. They descended the stairs and made their way to the back of the castle and the waiting fountain. When they approached she glanced around again, looking up to the walls and ledges, searching for the small creature.

"What did he say?"

Carlos stared at her for a moment, his face pale and blank. Her words had landed in his ears but had not registered.

"Carlos!" she said, shaking him stiffly. "What did Arias say?"

Carlos locked his gaze to hers slowly, taking two deep breaths before swallowing heavily. "He told me that Father will lead me into the woods at sundown. That he will most likely bring me near the pit before he, before he kills me." Carlos paused, remembering the cold metal against his back. "He gave me this." Carlos slowly pulled the blade free, not getting it an inch away from him before her hands shot out and pushed it back.

"Hide that!" she said, looking around frantically as he slowly tucked it under the back of his shirt again. "Are you mad? If someone sees that, or worse, Father..." She stepped back. "Word is already spreading. They are preparing your last meal as we speak. We only have a few hours left before..." Her words trailed off, sadness slowly working in as her own words resounded in her head... *Last meal.* There were so many things that she wanted to way, so many things that she was still too young to know how to express, or even understood herself. She knew that there was a strong chance that she could be losing a friend, the only one she had on the isle. She knew that if they succeeded, that if Carlos survived, that they would still be together, that they would have each other, but at this moment, standing in front of him a tear slowly worked its way down her cheek. She lunged forward, embracing Carlos tightly who gently wrapped his arms around the crying girl. Her tiny frame shook underneath his hands and he felt sadness welling behind his eyes. "Please be careful Carlos," she whispered into his shoulder. "I think Father suspects something."

Carlos squeezed her tightly, gently pushing her back to look deeply into her dark brown eyes. "Everything will be fine," he said, his words nearly convincing even himself that they were true. The truth was that he had no idea what was going to happen. The plan that he hadn't even convinced himself would work had already fallen apart, and now he was entering the woods alone with Father, and there would be no one to back him up when things began to unfold. Yet he stood, consoling the one person who gave him strength. He needed to show her that she was right, that he was brave; though at that moment, he felt anything but.

Isabella stepped back, wiping the salted lines that had formed with her sleeve. "There's something I want you to have," she said, reaching into a small pocket in her dress.

Her hand came back with a small photograph. "My Father took this in front of our house on his last visit; before we left."

Carlos took the photograph. In his hand, stood Isabella, bright and smiling, a black and white portrait of youth standing happily in front of a small Spanish style home.

He stood, searching for words, but they stayed

locked deep within, choked behind a welling urge to burst into tears.

"I'm going to follow you," she said suddenly, her words strong and unwavering. "When you go into the woods I'm going to follow you on the trail."

"No!" Carlos replied instantly, the sadness that had overwhelmed him moments ago now completely gone. "You mustn't. If Father finds you out there, you'll be killed; we'll both be killed."

"And if I stay here, and you don't succeed, then I'll just be waiting to die anyways." She regained her composure, the redness in her eyes highlighting the deep brown. "I have a friend, someone I know. Another girl that comes to the library every so often. She works in the kitchen. I can ask her for a knife and tell her that I need it for something I'm doing in the library. She won't think twice about it. I can't have you go into the woods alone. If the beast is as you describe, then you can't hope to defeat it on your own, and if Arias doesn't notice, or decides not to help. I can't allow it. I won't."

"Please," Carlos said, shaking his head slightly as he spoke. "I couldn't live with losing you because of me."

"And I can't allow my only friend to go into those woods alone to fight a monster."

Carlos could see by the piercing gaze locked to him and the stiffness in her reply that no matter what he said, her decision was already made and nothing he could say would change it. Again that warmth filled him. Slowly he nodded.

"We need to get back," she said, glancing towards the corner that led to the front. "We mustn't allow anyone to suspect anything. You need to pack your things and be ready to leave. I have some things I need to take care of, but be ready quickly."

Carlos nodded, taking a deep breath and exhaling heavily.

"Come on," she said, a smile working its way across her features. "We have a celebration to attend."

Carlos followed his friend to the front, slipping the photograph in his back pocket as they walked. When they entered the castle, he hugged her again as she made her way towards the library and then turned to make his way to his room. He packed in silence, pausing once in the middle to make his way to the window. For a short time he stood silent, peering across the grounds to the woods beyond. He knew the death they contained, and that there was a very good possibility that he was about to be added to those numbers. As he watched the light clouds drift overhead against the blue backdrop his mind wandered to Arias. He wondered if he and Isabella could live like that. Could they stake their claim on the island and create a home for themselves where they could live their days. He knew that would be impossible. Father would never stop hunting them, and that was not a life he wished, for him, or Isabella.

A short time later, the commotion in the hallway told him it was time. The celebration was beginning and his sending had begun.

THE SENDING

"This, is always the saddest of our days."

Dozens of eyes gazed across the dining hall, locked to the voice that echoed from the end of the room.

"When one of our own chooses to leave—to make their way back to the cruel world that once, had cast them out." Father's words echoed off the walls, reverberating through the room. "It pains me, because we are family. I know, that from this day forth, I will no longer be able to protect them, to shelter them from the murder, and violence that will be a plague upon them—the war and disease, hunger and grief that fills the world beyond this island. It is that which hurts the deepest." His gaze moved to Carlos. "When this young man first arrived here, we took him in. We opened our arms and our hearts to him. We showed him that there was a world, not filled with malevolence and hatred, but kindness and joy, a place where he could live out his days surrounded by companionship and endless feasts. Through us he learned to experience friendship and kindness. He learned what it meant to be accepted as part of a family. We could not have taught him a better lesson, a lesson which we hope will stick with him through his final days. I want you to know Carlos, that you are always welcome here. This will always be your home, and though none have ever accepted, I extend the same invitation to you; to return as I have all others who have left."

Carlos sat silent, the span of decaying bodies flashing past as Father spoke of those that never returned. He felt sadness welling in him, and a piercing contempt for the man who sat, lying behind a false mask of care.

Father's gaze moved back to the room. "You are all my children, to whom I dedicate my life. I nourish you, I give you shelter and warmth and I ask nothing in return, save for showing the same hospitality to your brothers and sisters. Now..." Father slowly stood, raising his glass in front of him.

Carlos felt disgust rising in his gut.

"Let us raise our glasses, and celebrate the life that Carlos has given to us, and his journey to what lay beyond the woods."

There was a slow murmur as the children raised their glasses, their eyes peering at the boy that many of them had only met in passing.

"Let us feast," Father said, taking his seat as the slow rumble that accompanied meal time filled the room.

Carlos' plate sat untouched, his hunger quelled by the driving nervousness that held his gut in an unrelenting vice. He chatted with Isabella and two other boys who asked him where he was going to go and why he wanted to leave. He found himself grateful that Isabella knew the answers quicker than he did. She had a way of being able to answer for him without making it obvious that he himself didn't know.

"New York!" one of the boys at the table replied, a thin line of spaghetti sauce dribbling down his puffy chin. "My ma always talked about goin there when I was younger, but Pa always said that the big city was no place for simple country folk like ourselves."

Another stared at him for a moment, thoughts working behind a judgmental stare.

"Well I think you're positively mental. This island is brilliant, and I for one, fully intend to stay here until I'm old and grey and well off my rocker."

"Well I think it takes courage to leave," Isabella said, a defending tone rising in her words that kindled the soft warmth in Carlos's chest. "I think it's brave of you."

Carlos looked at her and smiled sheepishly, feeling a hot glow moving to his cheeks.

The group chatted for some time before the room began to empty, the other children making their way back to their daily activities. When the two boys they had been speaking with excused themselves, Carlos nodded to Isabella and stood up, turning to make his way out.

"Carlos," Father called as he made his way towards the exit. "Say your goodbyes my son," he said as he turned to face him. "And when you are finished, meet me at the iron gates. I have prepared your travels and will lead you to the dock when the sun begins to set. Make sure to have all of your belongings."

Carlos nodded, beginning to turn.

"And Carlos."

Carlos paused, turning his gaze again to Father.

"Please refrain from taking anything that you did not arrive with."

Carlos stared at him for a moment, a sick hatred working its way through him before nodding and turning to leave the room.

For the next two hours he sat in his room, waiting for the sun to begin its descent. His mind raced over the decision, and multitude of possible outcomes, ranging from his body being cast heartless and torn into the pit, to arriving at the docks to find there really were no boats. He began to feel loss, a sad hole, building as he thought of Isabella. He had never met anyone like her, someone that made him feel welcome and wanted, a person that shared a mutual kindness and respect with. Of everything, from his life before, to the moment he was at, he realized that it was her, that he would miss the most. He pulled the photograph of her from his pocket and let his gaze fall downwards to the small picture. The welling urge continued to build. Then he pulled his gaze away and allowed it to move to the window. Beyond the dingy glass he saw that a light orange had begun to spread its glow across the sky. He took one last breath, deep and heavy, and then made his way outside.

IT BEGINS

The hall leading from his room to the entrance of the castle felt longer than it had in the months he had traveled before. The paintings on the wall seemed to lose their luster, faces watching with contempt as he moved quietly past. He felt the lifeless calm of the corridor and the cold stone beneath his feet, every crack and scuff mark standing clearly against the smooth polish surrounding it. The castle seemed darker—heavier, the distant laughter filtering past hollow and thin.

"Carlos…"

He turned to see Isabella approaching him.

Needles prickled across his skin as he felt the world around pressing in against his chest. As she approached the cold hollow inside grew. He searched for words, anything that could comfort the look on her face, but was left standing there silently.

She approached and embraced him.

Neither of them spoke, and when she pulled away, for a short time, they stared into each other's eyes, their gazes a voiceless conversation.

"Please be careful Carlos," she said, her hands wringing together in front of her.

Carlos nodded, reaching out to take her hands in his.

Her palms were warm, a soft layer of moisture

fraught with worry.

"If I... If I don't return, I want you to know. You've been the best friend that I've ever had."

A tear formed at the corner of her eye and she embraced him again. Her body trembled as she clung to the one person she had grown to care about: to love. She held tightly, a gentle regret flooding past that she had not held him sooner. Together they stood, embraced in the hallway, the world around them a meaningless hum. Then Carlos pulled back.

"I have to go."

Isabella nodded, another tear working its way down her cheek as she watched her best friend turn and disappear through the front doors.

As Carlos made his way across the yard he could see Father standing just beside the iron gate; the massive spires standing slightly ajar. There was a group of children gathered nearby to watch as he was walked into the woods; a lamb led to slaughter. He slowly passed, nodding politely as they whispered amongst themselves. Then he approached Father.

"Are you ready my son?"

He turned one last time to gaze at the castle to see Isabella standing at the bottom of the main stairs when a shriek of rusted metal behind him startled him back to the path ahead.

He turned to Father and nodded.

242

"Well," he said, pushing the gate open further. "Then let the journey begin."

Carlos stepped onto the path that was slightly wider than the one leading into the woods from the log. He ignored the hushed murmurs of the children behind and let his gaze fall to the shrouded growth perforated by a single brown trail. The forest was alive, the sounds of birds chirping filling the air as small critters ran along the branches overhead, thin rays of sunlight catching across their light brown fur. Behind him the ancient gate creaked closed.

"It is a shame that you have decided to leave us," Father said from behind, his gaze moving through the trees as if admiring his surroundings—surroundings that he was all too familiar with. "I'm sure your friend, Isabella, is going to miss your company. You two had become quite the pair."

Carlos thought of his friend, an icy layer of antipathy forming as his friend's name fell from Father's lips.

"But as all the others have, I'm sure she'll find another that she will call her friend."

Carlos stayed quiet. He worried that if he said the wrong thing, it may upset Father, and he didn't wish to call forth that anger prematurely.

"It is not too late," Father whispered, unheard by the boy walking slowly ahead.

"She was the first girl that was ever my friend,"

Carlos said after a moment, knowing too, that the longer he could keep Father engaged in their game of verbal chess, the closer to the pit he would get, and the better chance he would have of Arias noticing them.

"I'm sure there will be plenty of girls in New York for you to make friends with. I hear that it is a very large city, and growing every day. Do you have any idea what you plan to do whence you arrive?"

Carlos carefully maneuvered his piece.

"Maybe I'll work at a library," he said, the path illuminating a short ways away where some of the growth overhead had been cleared by a falling branch. "It's peaceful. I like that."

"Yes," Father replied quietly. "It is."

"Do you ever plan on leaving the island?" Carlos asked, watching as a squirrel darted across the path ahead of them.

Father stayed quiet for a moment, taking a handful of steps before answering. "I have often entertained that idea, but I always arrive at the same conclusion. My place is here, and I know not what I would do if I found myself anywhere else. Who would look after the others if I were to leave? No. This is where I belong. There is nothing for me anywhere else."

Rays of fading sunlight filtered through the air, shimmering swirls of yellow and orange working through them as the pair passed through.

"I must say though. I still find it strange that you wish to leave so soon."

Carlos kept his pace.

"It wouldn't happen to have anything to do with you taking your, *excursions* into the woods would it?"

Carlos tensed, preparing himself to run.

Father watched the boy walking ahead of him; studied the way he moved and breathed in his scent deeply. "Well you should actually consider yourself very lucky. Others have not been so... fortunate, to make it back out."

Carlos could feel the man's gaze piercing into him from behind. He knew he needed to keep the conversation going, but fear had stolen his words. He took step after step, anxiety building inside him as he waited for claws and fangs to sink into his back. But only the sound of footsteps crunching softly followed.

They walked for another hour, Carlos leading the way down the path while Father followed a short distance behind. It was a short time later that Carlos realized that the woods had grown quiet, the bird chirps no longer sounding in the air, and the creatures no longer frolicked around them. A quiet calm had settled through the trees and a purple haze began to settle into the sky above. He realized they were close, and at that moment, that his were the only steps to be heard.

Slowly he stopped, turning around to see Father

standing a short distance behind, his gaze locked to the ground just in front of his feet. His chest was heaving, breaths coming short and deep. Above him a single star hung in the darkening sky.

"Father?" Carlos asked, staring down the path as the man stood silently in place, his gaze locked to the space just in front of him. "What's wrong?" he asked as a faint breeze tinged with death wafted past his nose. It was at that moment that he knew their trek through the woods was at its end. He felt his skin pull tight.

Slowly Father lifted his eyes, the iris's shifting from a deep hazel to emerald-green, a thin ripple from the inside outwards. "eeaarrgghhHHH, NooooOOO!!!" Father screamed as his body began to contort, fighting against the monster that now tore its way to the surface. His body shifted, muscles rippling beneath a skin that stretched and contracted. "All you had to do was stay..." he continued, his voice low and strained.

Carlos stood frozen, watching as Father shook, fighting with all his will against the monster that fought to emerge.

"Carlos," he hissed as his face began pull back like the skin was being stretched tightly from the back of his skull. Like someone was pulling with their foot in his back and two handfuls of hair, his face contorting, skin tearing as his lips peeled backwards. "Run..."

Carlos could see the clothing across Father's arms

and legs beginning to flex as the muscles beneath grew; ripples running rapidly beneath fabric.

The last of the sun's light cast across the trees, and then the yellow disappeared.

Father's head tilted back, his mouth moving forward as it began to open wide. Carlos watched as course, black hair began to grow from his skin and the flesh peeled back as the maw of the beast ripped through splitting cheeks.

He couldn't move. His feet were rooted to the soil as if Father's words were manifesting in a literal form. He had forgotten about the knife tucked into the belt behind his back, about Arias, about everything except the monster that was forming in front of him. Then the thought of Isabella making her way through the woods hit him full force and he turned, bolting down the path as fast as his legs could carry him.

He heard the beast's howl as he got a short distance away, and knew that the monster would be crashing down the path after him any moment.

"Arias!!" he yelled, his lungs beginning to hurt from the outburst. "Arias!"

He ran, the trees flying past him, the path getting darker and darker as night settled in around them. Then as his legs were about to give out, and he realized that their plan had failed and he was going to die, he saw the clearing ahead.

He pushed forward, fighting against the raging burn in his legs and darted as fast as he could towards the open space, stopping just in front of the pit, his arms teetering to keep him on the edge without falling in. He could hear the sound of the beast rushing through the woods towards him and prepared himself for the attack. He turned, fumbling desperately to pull the blade Arias had given him. As he heard the monster approaching he raised it up, holding it unsteadily in front of him, a last desperate attempt to save his life.

Then the creature appeared.

From a short distance away the beast stepped out of the trees, its jade eyes locked to him, a snarl rippling across its lips as the bluish black fur enveloping it rippled against the stagnant breeze. It stopped as it stepped from the heavy growth, just yards away from where Carlos stood.

"Foolish child," the monster hissed through trembled words, a wavering reminiscence of Father's voice behind the echo of a guttural growl. "You think you have planned this escape unnoticed? You think me to be ignorant? No boy, I saw you all along. As the demon that watches over you is my eyes, I saw your every move. You believe yourself to be the first? No... No one leaves this island. Not I, not you. We are *all* part of it."

Carlos raised the blade slightly, watching as the

beast's gaze locked to it for a moment. For an instant, he thought he saw the fur where Father's scar was ripple lightly.

"You cannot kill me boy," it growled, lips pulling back to expose the row of glistening fangs as a smile hinted at the edges of its mouth. "This island will never let me die..."

"You can't have us," Carlos replied, fear entwined with his words. "I won't let you."

Carlos stared, watching as what appeared to be a grin began to grow.

"That boy, is where you are wrong."

The monster stepped forward, dropping its shoulders low to charge. Carlos tensed. Then the creature's eyes shot open wide and it flinched forward with a loud snarl.

He could feel the sweat slicking the handle of the blade in his palms and watched as the beast spun around, the end of an arrow shaft sticking out of its back just below its shoulder blade. Then he saw Arias sitting on a low branch of a tree a short distance down the trail.

"You!!" the beast roared as another arrow pierced into its chest and Arias dropped from the tree, turning to run down the trail in the other direction.

The creature roared, forgetting about Carlos who stood frozen in place and charged through the trees after the boy who still eluded him.

Carlos took three breaths, the blade still shaking at the end of his grip. The other boy had injured the monster and he knew it was a matter of time before the creature killed him and returned to finish him as well. He couldn't return to the castle now, not ever, not as long as Father still walked. He had no choice. He had to follow.

Carlos let his arm drop to his side and took one deep breath, exhaling with a gust and then charged down the path after the monster, leaving his boyish youth hovering scared at the edge of the pit. Trees whipped across his face as he struggled to follow the broken branches and prints left by the fleeing pair in the darkness. After a few minutes he slowed to a stop, his hands moving to his thighs as he leaned forward to take in deep breaths of cool forest air. Then he heard a shout a short distance away.

He composed himself and continued quickly in the direction, a short time later reaching the edge of another small clearing.

Against a rock face stood Arias. He had one last arrow which he was fumbling to nock against the string. The beast was slowly approaching him, tearing the arrows from his chest as he did, a thin trail of blood spurting onto the ground with every shaft torn free. Carlos could see the growing trail of crimson beneath the clawed prints in the soil. The creature had taken over six arrows directly to the chest and was still closing in.

As Arias attempted to lock the last arrow into place the beast rushed forward, swiping him hard against the side of his head with his massive paw. Arias flew sideways, landing heavily in the dirt, crimson slashes already flowing with blood by the time the dust settled. He slowly began to step towards the downed child when Carlos did the only thing he could think to do. "Get away from him!" he shouted, his voice breaking into a partial scream.

The beast's gaze whipped back to him, the two emeralds shining in the night shooting immediately to where he stood. It snarled, the jade portals opening wider, pupils dilating as they locked to their new target.

Carlos held the blade in his hand, his knuckles white. He could see as the beast stepped towards him that the arrows had taken their toll. His steps were slower and he could see that the creatures breaths were coming shorter and shorter, a thin line of blood working from the corner of its mouth down its neck towards the ground.

The creature snarled, its lips pulling back to expose serrated fangs that glinted crimson in the fading light.

Carlos braced himself as the beast stepped closer. Then when he was in range of the massive paws the sound of wood piercing flesh squelched out and his gaze moved up to where the tip of an arrow stuck out from its neck.

Without thinking he brought the blade up and stabbed the creature in the chest. He pulled the blade free and stabbed again, watching as the beast stared at him, disbelief and shock flooding its canine-like face. Then its legs gave out and it fell to its knees.

Carlos stepped back, staring into the creature's eyes as it struggled to utter last words that were held back by the wooden shaft. Its eyes slowly dimmed and then the beast slumped to the side. He stared unblinking as its chest slowly came to a shuddered stop. For an endless moment he peered down at the monster that moments ago stood over him, death in its gaze. When he was content that the beast was not going to rise again to finish its task, he lifted his eyes to where the boy lay across the clearing. Standing next to the still youth was Isabella, her hand still wrapped tightly around the bow held in front of her, her blank gaze locked to the monster on the ground.

Carlos carefully stepped around the beast and made his way to her, taking the bow from her and dropping it to the ground. This time it was he that locked her into an embrace.

Overhead the sky began to shift, thick clouds forming as the last of the light began to fade, leaving them enveloped in an encroaching blanket of darkness.

"Look," she whispered, pulling her head back, her

eyes locked to the beast lying on the ground.

Carlos turned slowly, fear welling up in him as he readied himself to see the monster rising from the ground. He prepared to see all their planning and luck dissolved by the magic of the isle, but what he saw instead worked a peculiar calm through him. He saw the creature's fur began to bristle again, the hairs falling to the side and pillowing on the ground around the beast's still form. Slowly it morphed back into the naked form of Father, the wounds left from the arrows and blade standing out clearly against the light olive tan of his flesh. As the transformation became complete the man who had led him into the woods appeared at peace, lying curled on a blanket of ebony fur.

Carlos stared, watching the chest for movement, and then turned to Isabella, glancing at Arias as he spoke. "We need to leave. Is he..?"

She turned her attention to Arias, bending down to check for breathing.

"He's alive, but barely."

She looks back up at Carlos. "I don't think he can walk..."

"Help me lift him," Carlos said, bending down to take one of his arms and getting his shoulder under it. Isabella did the same, gently lifting the young man to his feet.

As they began to make their way back to the path

Arias stirred. "Is he..?" he began, his words trailing off with a pained cough as the slashes across his face burned to life.

"Yes," Carlos replied. "We have to get back to the castle. We need to gather the others, and get off this island."

Above, the sky became a swirl of dark greys and white, generations of storms held at bay now beginning to swirl into a frenzy.

The three made their way slowly through the woods, exiting back out through the iron gates to the surprised faces of the startled children on the grounds.

The woods had come to life, wind rushing through the branches above in shrieks and howls. Swirls of dead leaves and dirt tornadoed upwards, spiraling through the thickening air. Throughout the trek Arias faded in and out of consciousness, mumbling about the beast in the woods and trying to find his friend who had gone missing. Quickly as they could, they made their way back to the castle.

An hour later they pushed back the iron gate and stepped onto the castle grounds. A group of boys that had gone outside to inspect the sudden change of weather rushed forward, startled as they approached by the sight of the two children carrying another, and the condition of the boy. They ran up and paused, two of them immediately lending a hand and lifting Arias from them, leading him towards the castle where Isabella and Carlos followed closely.

"What's happening?" one of the boys asked. "I thought you had left. And where's Father?"

Carlos ignored the other's words, pushing against the rushing air next to Isabella. They walked as quickly as they could to the castle, making their way up the steps and into the safety of the foyer.

As the pair began making their way through, the structure began to shift. The paper lining the walls began to peel and crack, windows shattering and falling to piles along the base, and the wood that was moments before, polished and strong, began to splinter and crack. The once pristine creation began to crumble around them, floors splitting and chandelier's cracking as dull crystal fragments rained down to the floor in a shimmering mist. The entire castle was going from an immaculate palace of stained glass and polished tile, to a decrepit, long abandoned home that had seen generations of disrepair and neglect at the hand of the storm covered island.

"What's happening?" one of the children accompanying the trio yelled as the banister leading to the second floor splintered and fell apart in front of them.

"Gather everyone," Isabella yelled over the moans of the dying mansion. "We have to leave, now!"

"What about Father?" the older boy that Carlos had first met shouted again.

"Father's dead!" she shouted. "We need to leave! Now!"

BROKEN ILLUSIONS / THE ESCAPE

Arias waited in the grounds near the front stairs. One of the boys began using strips torn from an extra shirt to create makeshift bandages for his face after even in the state he was in, he refused to go inside. Carlos quickly accompanied Isabella to her room.

The hallways were a jumbled mass of fleeing bodies; children running in every direction as the castle continued falling apart around them. The pair made their way as quickly as possible to her room, dodging the children rushing past in a chaotic frenzy.

Isabella turned and rushed towards her room, Carlos just behind her as they made their way through the streaming swarm of panicked youths. They charged into her room where she yanked a small case from beneath the bed and began to pile her clothes and a small stack of books in. While Isabella quickly packed her things Carlos waited just outside the door. Children were rushing past and he could hear yelling about the sudden change in weather, and what was happening to the castle and why they had to leave. Chaos wrapped in an opaque veil of fear had warped the interior of the once lackadaisical halls. When she was finished she grabbed Carlos by the arm, looking around as the wood paneling in the hall cracked upwards, splintering one of the arches overhead and a thick cloud of dust dropped downwards.

"Let's go!"

Carlos gave a single nod of reply and turned to follow her down the hallway, shouting to the others to get out of the building as they passed.

"We need to get everyone to the boats," Isabella yelled, the children rushing in chaos around them.

Carlos stopped, his eyes locking to hers as panic built behind them. "What if there *are* no boats...?"

Carlos stood silently, not breaking her gaze even as a boy rushed past and bumped full speed against his shoulder, the load of silverware in his hands clattering to the floor around them.

"They will be there," she replied, reaching out to squeeze his shoulders. "They will be there..."

Carlos nodded, turning as they made their way through the foyer and down the main steps where a large group of children had already begun to gather.

"What's happening!?"

"Just stay close, and follow the others," Isabella answered to a young boy that couldn't have been past ten. "Everything is going to be ok, but we have to go, now."

The children around them erupted into a jumble of shouts and fearful murmurs as the number of gatherers grew.

"Past the gates," Carlos said, the image of Father lying face down in the dirt flashing forward. "We follow the trail to the beach beyond. If what Father has said is true, then there should be plenty of boats for us all. It's not safe here anymore."

"I don't wanna leave," another boy cried. "I don't want to go back."

Isabella looked at the frightened faces that stared at her and Carlos, looks of desperation begging for answers.

"We can't stay here. Without Father, the castle will fall. There will be no more food, no more shelter. Without him, this island will die, and us along with it if we stay. Please… We must go."

"Where's Father?" another of the gathered children asked.

"Father's dead. He was killed by the beast," she lied, not wishing to further complicate their quickly narrowing escape.

The children burst into panic, shouts and cries erupting between them.

Behind them more and more children made their way down the stairs. Some carrying things stolen from the mansion, others with bags full of food from the kitchen and dining hall.

When the last of the stragglers finally emerged, Isabella looked at the older youth. "Is that everyone?"

The boy looked at her and shrugged, his face

warped with a sad unsurety, the castle falling into further degradation behind them as the tall chimney that stood on the far-left side broke free and fell to the ground in a thunderous roar. "I don't know..."

The main stairs began to crack, weeds working their way unnaturally fast through the opening spaces while the children stared in horror at the massive building that slowly continued to erode.

"Help me," Carlos said, breaking the boy's gaze that had locked to the crumbling palace.

The boy tore his eyes away and reached down to help Carlos pick Arias up.

"We can't wait anymore," Arias whispered, one good eye affixed to him between the strips of cloth.

Carlos and Isabella made their way towards the twisted gates and the shrieking woods beyond. The wind beat at them, struggling desperately to blow them sideways and away from their escape. The trees swayed and creaked violently as their tops were beaten again and again by the rushing air that now swirled the island. The woods around them were a swirling chaos of whipping branches and frenzied leaves.

As the group funneled through the gate the castle continued to crumble behind. The fountain at its rear collapsed outwards as the main center piece fell forward into the basin, shattering the outer wall as it landed.

They made their way quickly through the trees,

many of the children shouting their fears of the monster in the woods and the unsurety of their destination. As they continued their way onward, the younger children in the group began breaking into sobs as they were pulled along.

Moments later they arrived at the place where the path passed the pit.

"What...?" the boy whimpered as they edged their way around the circle of death, his eyes falling to the body of Marianna at its edge. "It's impossible..."

"Father was the beast," Isabella said, glancing at Carlos as she explained in the simplest form what was happening to the boy at her side.

"Marianna..."

Shock had filled his words as dry tears worked their way invisibly down his cheeks.

"We will explain everything when we get to the boats," Carlos said as the boy slowly made his way past the corpses, his gaze locked to the scene below. "But we need to keep moving."

Others gasped in horror, some beginning to cry as they recognized the faces of those that had been led into the woods, a realization that none had escaped and that everything they had been told was a lie. The children realized at that moment the truth of what they were seeing.

The group continued on quickly, single file as the

trees closed in on their escape, blocking the light out above and lashing out at their faces as they made their way to the beach. Half an hour later the trees pulled back and the spanning ocean opened up before them, dark and shifting, a palate of ebony blues that blended seamlessly with the swirling sky overhead.

As they filed out onto the beach, they saw the dock that Father had spoken of. It was a single strip of wood slats that reached out ten yards, with a small handful of rowboats tied to each side.

Carlos looked at Isabella, relief flooding his gaze.

"Everyone, get in!" Isabella yelled above the howling gale.

Together with the help of two of the older children, they fit everyone into the boats. When the last of the frightened faces were seated in the boats, Carlos made his way down the line, unfastening the ropes that held the tiny vessels to the dock. Behind him Isabella and one of the older boys helped Arias climb into the last boat. Carlos untied the last line and climbed in next to her and began pulling the oars as hard as he could, rowing them as quickly as possible away from the island as the rolling waves that battered against their escape.

The tiny ships made their way out, the large island growing further and further away. The children had fallen quiet, the sound of waves brushing against the side of their boats fading all conversation to a lull, save for the quiet murmurs shared between them. Carlos and the other boy had fallen into a rhythmic motion, their oars slapping quietly against the sea one after another.

Sitting quietly in the boat Arias held his gaze locked to the spiraling abyss of darkened clouds swirling violently above the island, and out of his one good eye, watched as the top of the castle slowly toppled out of view.

WHAT LAY BENEATH

The island had calmed, its initial rage finally smoldering to a gentle growl. Darkness still held its grip over the isle and a cold breeze flowed through the trees, brushing leaves past the still corpse of the man lying in the dirt. A short distance away the castle stood silent, a derelict shadow of its former self, abandoned and uncared for, for what seemed to be centuries, walls open and exposed as brick and mortar lay in piles at its base. The roof had collapsed at the rear and the grounds around it were now thick and overgrown, broken turrets covered in clinging vines. Mist drifted down through the open cavity above, casting a thin layer that glistened in the filtered moonlight.

Inside a tiny shape flittered unnoticed through the exposed foyer. It made its way past the splintered railing and stairs that had crumbled beneath as its tiny wings beat against the stagnant air, sending the occasional whisper of an echoed flitter off the fractured walls. The creature made its way past paintings that had cracked and curled inwards, frames left warped and brittle. It flew past the dining hall, the smell of must—a rot long past, wafting by as it passed. It flittered lazily above dust covered tables lined with remnant of fruits and other unrecognizable memories scattered across the tarnished serving plates. As it made its way down the hallway leading to the second floor the earth beneath began to shift, swirls of still dirt moving to life as tiny spirals of dust lifted to life.

It traveled silently down the hall, instinctually following the path of the stairs up to the second, the third, and finally, the fourth floor. As it did a translucent shimmer covered the halls, a ripple in its wake as the curls in the wallpaper began to disappear and pieces of broken glass reformed, shifting autonomously on the floor where cracks had begun to seal themselves. When it reached the fourth floor it slowed. The hallway was still dark, the windowless black illuminated only at the stairwell. From there to the engraved door was ebony pitch.

The creature flittered to the door and paused, brushing its tiny, clawed hand slowly over the lock. There was a click and a thin gust of air billowed outwards as the door clicked open and dim light seeped into the darkened hall. A thin ripple of excitement worked over its scales.

Beneath, the mansion slowly began to rebuild, the bricks falling back into place, the fountain slowly falling into its upright position.

The tiny creature began to flutter its wings furiously, its legs braced against the doorframe as it strained to pull the door open enough for it to enter the room. When the door finally budged with an unforgiving creak, it made its way in. The room was lit with candles that glowed immortally atop their wrought iron sconces, the light shimmering across the dull green of the creature's scales as it crossed to the center of the room. It fluttered through the air, landing on a small table with a crimson cloth embroidered in gold. The cloth monolith stood in the middle of the table, barren of all other objects. It stared at the shrouded shape for a moment as if studying it, its thin tongue flicking at the air between it as its tiny head cocked to the side in a series of silent mechanical clicks. Then it slowly reached out, pausing just before the cloth, took it in its hand and slowly pulled it back.

Standing in front of the creature was a clear glass container, slightly domed at the top with a crystal knob at its precipice. It sat plain against the decorated backdrop of the room. Inside sat a small ornate pedestal with a red velvet pillow atop it. On the pillow sat a human heart, a child's.

The creature stared at the still organ for a moment before closing the space and reaching out, pausing for the hint of a moment and then tapping a single claw against the glass.

Nothing happened.

It cocked its head to the side again, its wings flickering across its back for a moment before a single sound filled the room with a faint whisper; a breeze escaping from a hidden portal on the far wall, a whisper concealed in the air.

The creature flicked its gaze towards the sound and paused, a single twitch coming from its wings. Then it slowly rose into the air and made its way towards the wall.

When it reached the opposite end, it lit a small shelf. It walked towards the end, tiny claws clicking on the thick wooden surface. It approached the candle sconce that sat at the end and stopped. For a breaths time it stared at the flickering flame, the light dancing dully across its black eyes before leaning forward and extinguishing it with a single puff of breath.

Click

The panel next to the shelf slowly moved outwards, just an inch, a passage hidden perfectly behind the wall.

The creature flickered again, rising into the air and setting down just at the base of the door. It pushed itself through the crack and peered into the tunnel beyond. Leading downwards was a stone passageway, just wide enough for the tiny creature to fly through. It buzzed its wings for a moment and then started downwards, the light fading behind it.

It continued down for quite some time, the smell of damp earth swirling behind it, before the tunnel leveled out and began its way further inwards, to the heart of the island. Dirt filled the floor of the passage and more than once the creature had to stop and squeeze its way through where a root had grown through the wall. It was sometime later before a distant glow began to shine through the darkness.

It made its way towards the growing light, and as it began to illuminate its dull scales the passage opened up, a large cavern spreading out before it.

The room was massive, a sprawling castle beneath the ground. Stalactites hung heavy from the ceiling, a maw of dragon's teeth reaching downwards. Tiny crystals flickered in the light from a thousand candles that spread from one end to the other, wax dripping down to congeal in a thick carpet along the floor. In the middle of the room sat a small basin, no larger than a sink. Above it hung a copper pipe, a green tube stretching up into the ceiling. Beneath it a single drop of crimson dripped into the stone vessel.

"You must find another."

Words reverberated deeply from across the massive cavern, a sound wrenched from the bowels of hell itself.

"We must begin again."

The tiny creature rose into the air, flitting its way to the rim of the basin before landing and peering inwards.

Just beneath sat a small pool of burgundy liquid, its metallic scent rising into the air.

Another drop fell from the end of the pipe, the last remaining essence from Marianna's body above making its way downwards.

There was a large shuffle as the concealed horror stepped from the shadows, massive horns falling first to the light, followed by a leg tipped with cloven hooves and leathery skin, dark and crimson, matched by the last drop falling from the pipe." For a millennia I have existed, and for a millennia I will go on. As long as blood flows through the veins of the children, this island, and I, will continue." The demon growled deeply, its bat-like features twisting as its words reverberated off the distant walls.

The tiny creature atop the basin knelt, bowing its head deeply as the giant monster continued to speak.

"You will find another to take his place," it spoke as the candlelight illuminated the last of its features, a serpent tail flicking against the floor as it came to a stop. "A thirst must be quenched." The demon's eyes fell upon the basin, its pupils narrowing to serpentine slits as it focused on the single drop hovering at the edge of the pipe. "Go."

The tiny creature rose into the air, disappearing into the passageway leading upwards as the being beneath the isle took its last step towards the basin.

Above, through dozens of feet of earth and soil, sat decades of decay, the sprawling pit nearly fifty feet deep, filled with the countless corpses of those that had never escaped, those that had died to quell the unending thirst of the monster hidden beneath, in the heart of the isle.

END

www.ingramcontent.com/pod-product-compliance
Lightning Source LLC
Chambersburg PA
CBHW031611240626
47153CB00002B/714